Zero
at the
Bone

Also by Michael Cadnum

Calling Home
Breaking the Fall
Taking It

Zero at the Bone

Michael Cadnum

Grayslake Middle School
David B. Duffy
Learning Resource Center
440 North Barron Boulevard
Grayslake, Illinois 60030

Viking

VIKING
Published by the Penguin Group
Penguin Books USA Inc., 375 Hudson Street, New York,
New York 10014, U.S.A.
Penguin Books Ltd, 27 Wrights Lane, London W8 5TZ, England
Penguin Books Australia Ltd, Ringwood, Victoria, Australia
Penguin Books Canada Ltd, 10 Alcorn Avenue, Toronto, Ontario,
Canada M4V 3B2
Penguin Books (N.Z.) Ltd, 182–190 Wairau Road, Auckland 10,
New Zealand

Penguin Books Ltd, Registered Offices: Harmondsworth,
Middlesex, England

First published in 1996 by Viking, a division of
Penguin Books USA Inc.

1   3   5   7   9   10   8   6   4   2

LIBRARY OF CONGRESS CATALOGING-IN-PUBLICATION DATA
Cadnum, Michael.
Zero at the bone / by Michael Cadnum.
p.   cm.
Summary: When eighteen-year-old Anita fails to return home
from work, her parents and younger brother try to understand
and cope with her disappearance.
ISBN 0-670-86725-X (hardcover)
[1. Family life—Fiction.   2. Missing persons—Fiction.]
I. Title.
PZ7.C11724Ze   1996
[Fic]—dc20   95-50145   CIP   AC

Printed in U.S.A.
Set in Univers

For Sherina

Even with my eyes closed:
the tree so full of birds

1

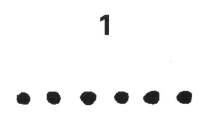

I smelled fire.

The first thing I tried to do was find my dad. It wasn't that easy—everyone in the mill looked the same, all snowy with cottonwood dust. Everyone wore white face masks and an improved kind of goggle ever since Leo lost an eye wearing the legally approved type of guard the day before Christmas two and a half years ago. Besides, no one could hear in there, the saws ripping up the timber so loud the workers wore ear protectors, green plastic earmuffs. You couldn't hear a scream.

So I hurried through the cabinet room, people stapling together nightstands. The hoses that powered the staplers hissed and the compressor thrummed so loud it shook everything inside my body, all my organs, the yellow air hoses wiggling, looping through the air.

I hurried into the office, hoping Dad was in there on the phone, but the only person there was Barbara.

She was standing in front of the copy machine. She had just got the front of the copier to come off, and was looking down at a paper jam, a bad one, several sheets of paper crammed into each other. Barbara is a caved-in kind of person who expects this sort of thing to happen. She was holding the entire front half of the copier like she didn't know what to do with it, put it down or put it right back where it belonged and forget she ever saw the big white cauliflower of paper in the middle of all those rollers.

"Where's Dad?" I said.

As soon as I said it, I knew it sounded a little unprofessional, the boss's son needing to talk to his father.

Barbara gave me one of her vague looks. "Hi, hon," she said. Then my question worked its way into her, and she said, "I think he's in back on the spur, but I don't know."

This was bad news in two ways. If he was back on the spur, he was up in the boxcar, supervising. The railroad spur brought lumber to the back of the factory, and I could make it there in half a minute, but I'd have to get his attention, forklifts rumbling and shouting guys all over the place. If he wasn't up in the boxcar, he could be anyplace, and I'd be way in the back of the furniture factory, about half a mile from the nearest phone.

Besides, I wasn't sure. If I had been sure, I would have punched 911 into the phone right there in the office. But I wasn't. I didn't want to believe it, that was part of the problem. Another part was that I was glad to be able to help Dad take care of things now that the nightstands were starting to ship out, and I didn't want to make a huge blunder my first week on pay-roll.

So I hustled back, through the cabinet room, air hoses bobbing overhead, all the way back into the mill, workers white with hardwood sawdust, the air thick with the bitter smell of the wood. I found the place right under the hole in the ceiling, where you can feel the fans drawing up air, and I told myself I was wrong.

There wasn't any fire.

No fire. Nobody else noticed a thing. Of course they wouldn't, their faces masked, each worker concen-trating on carrying the big, white, hairy boards, let-ting the saw take them, the air trembling with the shriek of the wood when the big saws ripped into them. I knew I shouldn't be in that room without ear protectors. Several spare ear guards hung on a hook, lightly dusted with sawdust.

I could run, now, and spread the alarm. But I didn't. I stayed, praying I was wrong. Up on my tiptoes, try-ing to argue with my own sense of smell. Trying to outsmart what I already knew.

There were red-and-white fire alarm buttons all over the factory, maybe even those fire extinguishers behind glass. All I had to do was kick the glass and the fire department would be here in record time.

But I could not see them. I saw useless, vivid details, a paper mask on the floor, its strap broken, the big sign, DAYS SINCE AN ACCIDENT: 940. I could see the hood off one of the lathes, the workers bent over the naked, still core of the power tool. They turned, glad to have a little downtime, smiling to see me. Their smiles went a little dead when they saw my expression.

It's amazing how that happens, people in the middle of routine, and then they know something is wrong.

This time when I rushed into the office, Barbara was crouched down by the copier, not even looking up, and I sat at her desk, her chair still warm. I could turn on the intercom and make an announcement, ask for my dad by name, as though he could hear me all the way inside the Southern Pacific car. I could push the buzzer for five o'clock closing time, although it was only four-fifteen. I could punch a series of preset numbers, call my mom, or Anita, or Dr. Pollock.

But I had to stop and think before I found the button for an outside line. I don't know why they decided 911 was a good idea. It doesn't matter now. But I think they might have thought about choosing 211, which would be easier.

Or even 111. And then when I was done, I pushed the intercom button and kept my voice slow and steady. "Mr. Buchanan, front office, please." This meant that someone on a forklift would hear me and get my dad's attention and tell him Cray was on the intercom, and in about five minutes my dad would get done taking care of whatever he was doing. Dad loves to work and he hates to be interrupted.

I found one, right by the women's lavatory, a big red Kidde fire extinguisher, and I tucked it under my arm. It was like running with a torpedo under one arm, a strange new game, half football, half war. I knew it was a little useless. Spray from an extinguisher like this would not reach up into the chute, past the fans, into the burning sawdust up in the hopper on the roof.

Jesse, the foreman, looked up from the lathe and ran after me, and he didn't even have to ask. Jesse can move fast. He hit the switch on the wall, and shut the fans down, the room falling still, the saws going from monster soprano to dull steel moan to nothing. So silent.

Jesse was under the chute, looking up, and he looked at me after I joined him, the fans slowing down, big propellers between us and the sky. Jesse is wide and tall, with ebony skin and a close-clipped black mustache. "Better get your dad," he said.

Smoke was sifting down, now that the fans were still. The gray fumes drifted, like something that was supposed to happen, a celebration everybody had planned, little charred specks of confetti.

2

The nearest fire station was on Fruitvale, only a few blocks away, and the sirens started up fast and then seemed to linger in the near distance, the sound hanging in the air. It was like all those other times when a siren has passed on the edge of my attention, nothing to do with my life or the life of anyone I love.

It was only as the siren grew closer that the thrill of it, and the fear, began to take hold of me again. The siren reached a crescendo and the sound of the engine was right outside.

Their footsteps shook the floor. The firefighters filled up the entire front entrance, marching through the front door into the office. Barbara was making one of her "don't look at me" expressions, one hand held out. Giants in black waterproofs and helmets clumped up to the counter where the UPS packages, Jiffy bags of touch-up paint, were piled.

One of them carried an ax. A bright steel ax with a red stripe up the side of the blade, and a sharp hook at the other end of the ax head. All I could think was—they're going to tear holes in my dad's factory. And I had better be right—there better be a fire.

"It's in the sawdust hopper," I said. "On the roof."

Then I shut myself up. Here I was, talking like I knew what I was saying, and the firemen looked at me, their visors tilted. Their faces had open, tense expressions. They were ready for a fire, but it was all right if the fight was easy. I half expected the head firefighter, an especially tall man, my size, to tell me I was too young to know very much—they wanted to talk to someone in charge.

But the tall fireman asked where the quickest access was, from the side street, or from somewhere inside the property. I told him I thought the side street was probably a good idea. And they left. They didn't bump into each other, scrambling. They were there, and then they were gone.

Barbara gave me a round-eyed expression. Her finger was pointed at the phone, ready to start punching numbers on the intercom, the telephone, but she didn't know what to do.

I tore outside, and ran faster than I had ever run before, faster than the time I ran for eighty yards and a concussion in the game against Skyline.

My dad was already on his way, and he can run. He pointed up to the roof with one hand, and he was running so hard his arm waved up and down a little.

By now smoke was rolling out of the top of the hopper, a funnel-shaped structure on top of the roof. Fire-fighters were taking their time getting up the ladder, making sure the ladder was steady, making sure their feet were in the rungs.

"Clear the finishing room," my dad said.

He said this without looking at me, but it was me he was talking to.

The finishing room was always a dream world, blue and pink chairs hanging from hooks in the ceiling. The floor was uneven with paint of all colors, as though a volcano of party colors had erupted once years ago.

The workers were spraying banana yellow just then, the stuff coming out thick. A bentwood chair hung there in the air and a worker aimed a nozzle at it and the blond, bare wood was suddenly clotted with paint, the stuff not cut thin enough to go through the gun, the metal nozzle a space weapon that didn't kill, it just made things change color.

If the factory roof began to burn, this place would explode. Barrels of black paint labeled FLAMMABLE lined a wall. I called out that everyone should go outside, there was a fire. Maybe I expected panic. People finished what they were doing. An air compressor stuttered into silence. Someone untied a smock and let it fall, but you would have thought I had just announced an extra coffee break, or closing time forty-five minutes early.

I wanted to jump up and down and tell them the paint they were spattered with was loaded with ketones and other chemicals that would burn white hot, but they all wandered past me, cheerful, saying, "How's it going, Cray?" and things like that.

At times like this, I felt my inexperience. This was the real world. Workers were used to this. A disaster could erupt, and they all accepted it. I was too new to stay calm, to saunter out through the sliding wooden door, peeling off a glove, looking around at the fire hoses kicking as the water pressure stiffened them, like all of this was an everyday affair.

For a few minutes the hopper was the center of activity, fire helmets bending down over it, my dad on the roof in his short-sleeved blue shirt. The smoke turned into steam, a hose sprang a leak, fine spray fuming out from the socket where it joined the hydrant.

The ax flashed. A gentle splintering sound reached the street.

Water pattered down into the mill, and workers put down buckets and plastic tubs to catch the water and then gave up, putting tarps over the saws. The drops of water blistered the sawdust that covered everything like a coating of eraser crumbs. The workers were on overtime now, the few who were left, and I was going to be late for my meeting with Coach Jack unless I hurried.

There was no smoke, only the scent of charcoal and the perfume of wet sawdust.

My dad trotted out through the mill, gave a quick order to one of the workers, and then he was gone. He was the only one in a rush now. I ran to catch up with him and reached him just outside the huge, metal-ribbed boxcar. It's easy to forget how big a railroad car is. In movies people jump up onto boxcars or roll out of them. I could not approach this warehouse on steel wheels without thinking how dangerous it would be to jump into one if it was traveling hard.

"I have to go," I said.

My dad scrambled up into the car, and looked down at me. The interior of the car was stacked with lumber, and there was a forklift inside the boxcar. It was one of my favorite visions, the way one forklift would lift another into the interior of the rail car, one yellow machine cradling the other like a tractor that had given birth.

"Tell Mom the shipment got here from Alabama and I have to unload." He usually called her Fran here at the factory, even when he was talking to me, keeping our home life separate.

I really had to talk to him. I had to say something, it didn't matter what, and hear his answer.

When people were cut at the factory, they didn't howl or get angry. They made their way out into the office and asked Barbara for the first-aid kit. If the cut didn't stop bleeding, Jesse drove them to the clinic.

And even though the sign announced the number of days since the last accident, the accidents referred to were major accidents—a broken bone, the loss of something that wouldn't grow back, like what had happened to Leo despite all precautions, or like what had happened when my dad had just bought the place from Mr. Ziff, when Ziff Furniture was famous for its children's furniture and nothing else.

I thought about it sometimes: I hoped I would never have to do what my dad did that time, running back into the factory for something that had just been cut off. I couldn't help it: the fire had scared me. I needed a little reassurance.

"Everything's going to be all right?" I asked.

"Sure." It was one of my dad's characteristic *sure*s.

Then he turned back and gave me a smile, looking down, and I could see the sudden shadows under his eyes. And I could see how guilty he suddenly felt, giving me a such curt response. "You did fine, Cray. Really good. Another couple of minutes and we would've had a five-alarm disaster on our hands."

That was what I had needed to hear. And I also needed to see him turn to the stack, the pale lumber stenciled GEORGIA PACIFIC in fuzzy blue lettering. He climbed into the seat and gunned the forklift, everything back to normal, the boxcar filling with bad air.

3

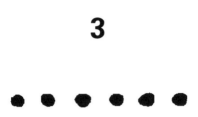

I was late getting the number 46 bus up Fruitvale to MacArthur, so I ran all the way. It's a long run, but I needed it, letting each stride burn off some of the left-over tension. I was a little out of shape, and I got sweaty inside my clothes.

Most people have jobs and they either like the job or they don't. They get up, work, look forward to vacation. Both my parents have jobs they love, jobs they care about the way people care about gardens they plant from seeds in a packet.

I already knew what Coach Jack was going to ask me, and I knew what my answer was going to be, in spite of the fact that crossing the football field gave me that wonderful feeling. The stripes every ten yards were faded, the chalk crumbled away, dirt and dead grass showing through.

One of the school district gardeners had tried to make the sidelines more permanent, a long, straight line burned into the field with an herbicide. The grass died, but didn't vanish, just turned a lurid orange color. It was the kind of thing nobody talked about, but I thought people would be glad when football began and the dead stripe was covered over by a thick chalk line. Something about the orange grass looked like science gone awry, like someone who tried a new dye on his hair and it came out all wrong.

There was no way I was going to play football this year. Not the way things were. I had been a pretty good quarterback, the junior varsity team winning four in a row at the end of the season. I was proud of that.

But a Skyline defensive back had nearly fractured my skull last year, and the varsity team had two fine quarterbacks. Coach Jack would extol the manly virtues of being third string, and tell me he needed a punter or another wide receiver. I liked football—and I hated it.

Coach Jack had one of the few offices with an outside door. It was a metal door, heavy, something you'd expect in a bomb-proof bunker. I'm not weak, but I had to wrestle against the power of this barrier.

Coach Jack had pictures all over his bulletin board. He is a private man; you can't read his eyes. So, to compensate, he put up a permanent display in his office. You could tell things about him without having to ask. They were mostly black-and-white glossies,

Coach Jack in a UCLA jersey, looking young and smiling. It was one of my dad's rules: "Don't smile too much; it makes you look nervous."

One picture showed a player upside down in midair next to another player who was in the air, too, right side up. This photo was going yellow, deep yellow, almost brown. Immanuel Jack takes a hit from Cal Bear Preston Harr. Immanuel Jack was hanging on to the ball. You couldn't see his face, only his helmet, the interior all shadow, like there was no one inside. A big, full-color photo showed Coach Jack not smiling nearly so much in a Dallas Cowboys jersey.

Coach Jack was listening to the radio, one of those fancy devices, shortwave, weather channel, AM/FM. He turned it off as soon I finished wrestling the door. Before I caught my breath, before I could even sit down among the piles of blank attendance forms, he said, "Merriman shot himself."

I knew what the words meant, but the actual, real-time meaning did not make any sense. I moved the attendance forms, put them neatly on the floor, and sat down. Bad news hits me like this—I have to do something to work off some of the shock.

"My starting quarterback," said Coach Jack. He added, quietly but definitely, "Bang."

I must have looked stupid. I hate that, when you don't have time to get the right expression on your face.

"Right in the foot with a twenty-two automatic," said Coach Jack.

"That's awful," I said. It was the kind of news I can't take in all at once.

"He's lucky," said Coach Jack.

If invaders bombed and blew up the entire city of Oakland, destroying every dwelling, Coach Jack would say: We're lucky. He would mean that it could have been worse, that it was a good thing more people weren't killed. But Coach Jack's concept of good luck is a little dry for most people.

"A thirty-eight is no joke," said Coach Jack. "Makes a big crater. A twenty-two pistol leaves just a little bitty hole."

I was still having trouble with the news. "But he won't be able to play quarterback this year."

Coach Jack gave me one of his classic looks: got it in one.

"Because bullet wounds are more serious than people commonly realize," I said, wanting him to know I had stayed awake for the California Police Officers Association film that rainy day early in my junior year. It bought me some time, making conversation.

"Merriman will not play football this year," said Coach Jack. Merriman as a quarterback was a work of art. The backup varsity quarterback was a guy named Allen Shelly. He was good. Not better than me, but so mean-spirited he willed things to happen. If Shelly threw a ball, receivers caught it out of fear of what Shelly would do to them if they dropped it.

Coach Jack opened a drawer and pulled out an Oakland Unified School Sports Release form.

"Shelly's in trouble," said Coach Jack, rolling the form up into a wand.

"What else is new," I said, a nonquestion.

"He got arrested again," said Coach Jack.

"Shelly has one of those complicated lives," I said.

"Charges got dropped, because the store owner had a heart attack. But Shelly's family decided enough is enough." All this with little pauses between phrases, the release form rolled so tight it was a blank white shaft.

I was supposed to say something, make conversation at this point, but I didn't speak.

"He's not coming back," said Coach Jack, and he gave this statement a certain weight. "He moved to L.A. to be with his dad."

"Long Beach," I said. Shelly had spent summers and Christmas down there and had bragged about breaking someone's arm in a fight on Lakewood.

Coach Jack smiled. This was so rare that I marveled at how different it made him look, suddenly handsome. Older-looking because of all the strange wrinkles around his eyes, but handsome. "So you are now starting quarterback. If you want it."

I had so much feeling I couldn't even look at him. It wasn't a question of want. I enjoyed almost everything about football, and the chance to spend the fall of my senior year playing a dream position made it hard for me to sit still. I stood and looked out Coach Jack's tiny, metal-mesh window. I set aside my fear of the game. Fear was nothing compared with this opportunity. I had expected the coach to offer me a backup assignment, something easy to pass up.

The window had been washed recently, one little wedge of scum at the bottom the squeegee had missed. This time of year the sun stayed long into the evening, and a man and a dog were racing. The dog had the man beat easily, but he was holding back, letting the man stay even with him, for the sport of it.

"It's something to think about," I said. I didn't like the prospect of getting a brain bruise, but only a pure coward would pass up a chance like this.

After my concussion my mom had shut herself in the upstairs bathroom and cried, stuffing her head in a towel or a pillow so I couldn't hear it. But I could. I sat there on the sofa with an ice pack on my neck watching an old Humphrey Bogart movie with my dad, but I could hear every sob she made, all the way inside me.

"That's what I want you to do," said Coach Jack. "I want you to think."

It was the way my parents felt that stopped me from agreeing right there in the office. My dad never wept, but he had been told to sit up with me and make sure I didn't throw up or fall asleep. He stayed up with me until three o'clock in the morning, even though Mr. Ziff was paying one of his rare visits to his former factory the very next day.

Coach Jack got up, putting the form on the desk, where it stayed rolled up, rocking for a while before it was still. He stood looking at a special picture on the bulletin board, one I didn't like to pay attention to. "I can't put pressure on you," said Coach Jack. "I think that would be wrong."

The photo he was looking at was of a car completely smashed, ripped in half, bits of car everywhere. Was Coach Jack being sneaky-smart, letting me know he knew about injuries and pain? Or was he being flat-out fair?

"How long do I have before I decide?"

My sister Anita said that football players put on a big show of being cartoon characters, animated creatures who can't be hurt. Anita would sit on the sofa next to me and watch a football game sometimes and smile when I cheered a spectacular pass. She would come back into the room from a phone call saying, "What's the score now?" trying to share the excitement. But Ping-Pong was her game. She and I would set up the green table in the backyard and play for hours. Sometimes Anita's serve wasn't very good, but once she warmed up, she knew how to put spin into the ball. The two of us would play far into the dusk, laughing, unable to see the ball but playing anyway, we could anticipate each other's game so well.

Coach Jack looked right at the wreck that had stopped his career, like the photo had nothing to do with him.

"Besides," he said, "your parents will have to sign the release form."

The permission form, he meant—the one indicating that it was all right for me to play a sport where players got a fifteen-yard unnecessary roughness penalty for tearing off an opponent's head.

"You have a special talent, Cray. You know what it is."

It's something I don't like to talk about, and it isn't simply that I can run or throw: I'm not a bad person. But people trust me in ways I don't ask for. The last four games of jayvee football we played in terrible rain, three of the games away games, nine people in the stands, nobody caring what a bunch of sophomores and juniors did on a muddy field. And I felt the strangest joy. We could win. Even on that last, blown play, offensive linemen swimming in muck, I knew the game was ours and all I had to do was run down the field all the way for a score.

And I did. Coach Jack had a picture of it, right there next to a faded bell schedule from last year: me staggering into the end zone with the ball, even though I was out on my feet, unconscious, the same as dead but stumbling forward for six points.

He took out a tack and put the tack in again, right in the same hole in the corner of the picture.

4

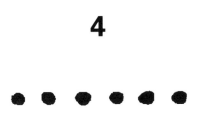

Our dishwasher leaves little specks on the dishes, dried-on white freckles. I scraped a rice scab off a fork with my thumbnail as I told Mom about the fire.

"I wondered what this was," she said at last, picking a black fleck from my hair. She held it up on her forefinger. "The world's smallest charcoal briquette," she said. "Perfect for a flea's barbecue." She wiped it carefully on the corner of a napkin.

I was a little embarrassed. I would take a shower after dinner. "Dad's paying a crew time and a half to unload the boxcar."

"Derrick loves it." She called him by his first name like this when she wanted to hold him up to the light mentally, turn him around like a fascinating specimen. Sometimes she looked different when she talked about him, a soft look in her eyes. "Forklifts, fire engines."

"A spark probably got sucked up the ventilator," I said.

I had a plate in front of me, lasagna covered with Saran Wrap, the hot food fogging the plastic. Anita said the microwave probably permeated the food with toxins from the plastic.

Mom was eating broccoli and French dressing, dipping the broccoli florets into the dressing, rolling them around, and chewing them slowly. She had lost thirty pounds over the last few months, although she still had dimples in her elbows when she put them on the table.

"Why are you looking at me like that?" I asked.

"Like what?"

"Like you're thinking about doing research on my head."

"Just wondering if you have any more black specks in your hair." She got up and opened the refrigerator, pouring some sparkling water into her Betty Boop glass. Anita and I had shared the price of a Swiss-made Betty Boop wristwatch on one of Mom's birthdays. The watch was water-resistant to one hundred feet, but Mom kept it on her dresser next to the photo of her parents.

"Where's Anita?" I asked. What I meant was, Let's not talk about my head. But I knew my mother didn't want to take the news about the fire seriously. The time my grandfather was in the hospital with pneumonia my mother had cold sweats and a headache, the worst migraine of her life.

"She has that new job," Mom said.

"I thought she was baby-sitting with Kyle," I said. This was a little snotty of me because it was my theory that Anita took baby-sitting jobs so she could grope in the dark with Kyle while the toddlers lay deep in dreamland. I knew all about her new job, checking inventory for an office supply company, working evenings, correcting the mistakes the day people made.

"Kyle called," Mom said.

"Wonderful."

Mom looked at me. She does a lot of talking with her eyes. "We had a nice chat."

"This couldn't have been Kyle you talked to," I said.

She gave me a lift of one eyebrow. I had the Saran Wrap off the plate, and it turned out I was hungry.

"Dad was afraid we were packing some of the nightstands wet," I said.

"That's not a very good idea," she said.

"He had Jesse break open a couple of cartons before the truck came, and they looked okay." Most of them looked okay. One had a weird little wrinkle from being packed in a carton too soon. That item would have to be sanded and refinished. One of the men in the shipping department had a problem, and Dad kept him employed because he felt responsible for the man's family.

"You like that, don't you?" Mom said. "You're going to be talking about board feet and drawer pulls, just like Dad."

22

My mother worked almost entirely at home, drawing pictures of fossil bones. She had an office upstairs all to herself. She had a magnifying glass on a crookneck stand, and sat with a pair of tweezers and a fossil jaw or a tooth or skull and turned it over, nudging it with the tweezers, all the while her other hand was busy sketching front, back, and overhead views.

It's surprising how many of the fossil parts are pieces from some animal's head. Mom explained that this is because the lower jaw is the hardest bone in any body, and the cranial bones are almost as strong, and, of course, the teeth. Maybe this is why my concussion had a special impact on all of us, with a shelf full of fossilized head parts upstairs.

"We're making a profit," I said.

I liked saying *we*. For the first time in my life, my dad had let me into his world, even though it was only part-time, just for the summer, and my official job was assistant foreman, which meant I did what Jesse told me to do. Ziff Furniture had a big contract, fifteen hundred nightstands for a chain of motels headquartered in the City of Industry in Southern California.

"It's wearing him out," she said. "He comes home and falls asleep in front of the eleven o'clock news."

She never put it so nakedly. Sometimes she acted as though the factory was a slightly unnecessary preoccupation of my dad's, something he took up the way some husbands take up getting a pilot's license. I knew how she really felt, how worried she was about my father, how concerned that he might get injured, or get another ulcer like the one that Dr. Pollock could still see on the X ray, the scar like a ghost.

"Why doesn't Anita go back to work with Dad?"

"You know why," said Mom.

I did know, but it was sometimes hard to draw Mom into the conversation at the angle I wanted. It was hard to get her to talk at all, sometimes. You could rush in, say hello, talk about the weather, show her the mail that had just arrived, ask if there was any news on TV, and all Mom would do in response is give a little wave, one finger, like a little puppet. Then she would say something like, "You like to hear about disaster, don't you?" Sometimes it was as if she was an anthropologist. She was doing research on our family and, against the rules, had grown to love us.

She liked to be alone. If she was in her room drawing a fossil, it was a rule: Don't talk if you can't see me. It was the opposite of my dad, who had to be all over the place, talking to everyone, helping lift this, helping nail down that.

So I switched tactics, and decided to take Mom's mind off Dad, because I knew that was what bothered her. "Did you go by the university today?"

"Sure," she said. This was a habit she had picked up from Dad, and she gave a little laugh.

"So, are you going to be famous?"

She answered by moving one finger—this was a painful subject.

"Do you get to name the new species or not?"

"No news," she said.

"Why does it take so long?"

She gave a shrug—not like most people's, a shrug that expressed ignorance. She meant that the problem of whether or not she had discovered a new species of bay tree was an example of life's complexity, a tiny fragment, proving the big problems of existence. It was also her way of telling me that she was trying not to let it bother her.

"Maybe Dad and I should go in and lean on someone." I liked sounding like this, a tough guy. I was joking, but I knew if I wanted to threaten someone, I could.

Mom squinted at the broccoli stalk in her fingers, looking hard, like she had just discovered a new species of bug. "I don't know how much more of this I can eat."

"You look good," I said encouragingly. It was true. I like to cheer people up, but I don't believe in lying just to be nice.

She smiled. I had her full attention now, the way I had when Anita and I used to put on puppet shows for the family, Mom saying she wanted to see the part where Grandma punched the wolf in the snout one more time.

"You *could* go get the bay tree report," she said, "but it's in Anita's room."

I liked the challenge—could I slip into Anita's room undetected? It posed a slight ethical problem: I knew Anita wouldn't like me poking around in her room. She'd try to be polite about it, but my family made a big point of respecting each other's privacy.

But I was just stalling, not wanting to talk about what was on my mind. I knew how Mom would react, even though she had a way of surprising me, of laughing at the same stupid movies I did. She didn't usually mind when Anita and Dad got into one of their arguments. At times like those, Mom wasn't pretending to be above it all. I think she really liked the sound of the two of them debating the rights of trees versus human beings, while I couldn't stand hearing two people I loved getting furious about sequoias. It wasn't that Mom liked bickering—I think she liked hearing us talk for the same reason people like to hear birds chirping.

So I dared myself a little. Go ahead, I urged myself. Tell her you want to play football.

5

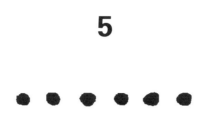

Mom had a tropical garden at one end of the living room, coffee bushes and sensitive plants, a mimosa that folds a leaf when you touch it. I knew this small, happy jungle was her territory, even though she would be happy to see me among the glossy coffee plants, enjoying them. My family had long since sectioned the house into private domains. No one would ever go into my room looking for a pencil.

So I hesitated. Anita's door swung open silently, but I didn't hurry in. I was about to break an unspoken promise.

Her room was very neat that evening, and this surprised me a little. It was never this well ordered. High on a shelf perched old toys, an old teddy bear worn free of fur everywhere except deep in his ears and under his arms. One button eye dangled. In two weeks Anita would be eighteen, and she had graduated from high school just a few weeks earlier.

It struck me how adult her room was, the refuge of

a grown woman, with a few relics of childhood and high school years kept around fondly, for historic reasons. Her plan was to take a year before she went to college, save up some money. The clutter of paperbacks and clothes I remembered from earlier years was gone. Kyle smiled from the top of her dresser, his graduation photo, blankly handsome like one of those pictures you see in barbershops, the kinds of hairstyles you can choose.

She still had her Ping-Pong paddles right where she could find them, the set with leather handles I had given her last summer. She had a filing cabinet on wheels, white, with a white handle. The blue plastic tabs on the folders were labeled—Resumes, Letters/Senate, Letters/Congress—but the files hung nearly empty. I was trespassing in her room, all the way across to her desk. Right beside the *American Shelf and Filing Employee Handbook* was my mother's report, with a yellow Post-it folded and stuck together as a bookmark. The yellow bookmark was between the last page and the cover, not really marking a place at all.

Arranged along one side of the desk was a series of five snapshots, pictures I had taken, Anita as she ran from the surf at Santa Cruz the summer before. I had snapped the camera as quickly as I could. She ran from the ocean, her light brown hair looking darker because it was wet, her T-shirt and cutoff jeans soaked through, a bra strap showing at her shoulder.

She ran toward the camera, and you could tell she was laughing at having her picture taken, getting closer and closer. In the last picture she posed a little, one hand on her hip. Anita wasn't someone who needed makeup. She had color, in her cheeks, her smile.

Something smelled new, fresh-from-the-factory. I found the source of the scent, a new pair of jeans, still stiff, folded neatly on a chair. I almost wanted Anita to come home early. I wanted her to burst into the room tugging off her sweater or hopping on one foot to peel off a shoe. I wanted to ask her how her job was going, and then I would tell her about mine.

Even that night, when he came home with his shirt-tail hanging out and his hair sticking up in wild spikes all over his head, he kept up a running patter, asking Mom how everything was, telling her the timber all got unloaded, telling her there was a fire in the hopper.

Mom didn't answer. She watched him, following him with her eyes, not trusting talk to tell her that he was all right.

"Lasagna," Dad was saying. "Two minutes on high," he said, poking the numbers on the face of the microwave. "Or, wait a minute; I don't want to nuke it crisp. Maybe medium high."

"How did it start?" asked my mother.

My dad was getting utensils out of the drawer.

"Fork, spoon, I don't need a knife." Sometimes I sneak up on him while he's in another room getting dressed or waiting for his cinnamon oatmeal to cook, and he's talking, quietly. Being around people makes him keep up a running stream, as though we were blind and wouldn't know what he's doing unless he tells us. But even when he's alone, he says things, patting himself, asking the empty room, "Where are the keys? What did I do with my belt?"

He sat across from Mom and peeled the Saran Wrap off the lasagna, and told her all about the saws, how they hit gnarls in the lumber and sometimes send up a tiny spark of hot steel. She knew all this, but she was brooding over the factory and looking at my dad, really seeing him. It made me look at him, too, seeing a man who was very thin, with gray in his hair, his glasses slipping down his nose a little as he ate. He pushed them back up with his finger.

"Jesse had nothing but praise about Cray today," said Dad, telling Mom as though I was in another part of the house and couldn't hear. "I'm not surprised," he said, and then he looked at me, smiling crookedly as he chewed.

One of the annoying things about my dad is that he will not clean his glasses even when they are dirty, and you have to look into his eyes through a snow of sawdust. People will do anything for him. The cabinet workers voted against striking a few months before out of loyalty to Dad, not wanting to hurt his chances with the nightstand contract. Maybe I inherited some leadership quality from him, but I knew I was imperfect inside. I didn't always say what I was thinking. Like now, I knew it was better to not mention football. I was even wondering if I could forge their signatures on the permission slip.

I could fake my dad's kangaroo scrawl, I was sure. But my mother has surprisingly delicate handwriting, very neat. I don't think my father would ever think like this—how to lie on a legal piece of paper. My dad is someone you can hear in a distant room, laughing. When he is in the kitchen alone reading the newspaper he makes sounds of surprise or annoyance.

My mother tugged his glasses from his face without saying anything. She washed them off at the sink while he blinked, gazing around, trying to make something out of what he saw. He looked at where he knew I was and said, "We'll have to have the ducts checked tomorrow."

She wiped the glasses very carefully with a paper towel. When she gave them back to him, she had a little smile, as though something private had passed between them.

I called Merriman from my room. I had picked out a red portable phone. I had figured a red phone would be easier to find. Now I wished I had a squat black one, like the ones detectives use in black-and-white movies. His sister answered, Kentia, a suave, cool freshman at Stanford. Kentia is a beauty. Even her name is special: *Ken-tee-yah*. When I told her who I was, she said, "Who?" Not because there was anything wrong with my voice or my name. She was too elegant to hear things the first time.

My room has pictures of stars and planets, posters that came in *The National Geographic* and others I bought at the Nature Company, novas, craters. Anita had once pointed out that it wasn't the infinite horizons of space I found intriguing, it was the residue of explosions. There was a silence, and muffled shuffling sounds, and I pictured Merriman on crutches, hunching his way to the phone.

Sometimes I have trouble with words. It's like coming right out and saying it makes it all worse. I felt myself wanting to blurt, I'm sorry you shot yourself in the foot. "Shelly moved to L.A.," I said, as though that was the reason I had called, not mentioning handguns.

"Do you know what pain is?" Merriman asked, not bothering to comment on a criminal like Shelly.

I wasn't really very interested in galaxies anymore. A picture I had put on my wall more recently was a picture of the last man to play in the National Football League without a helmet. The photo was one I had blown up at Copymat out of a book on the history of the sport. He was being led off the field with a grimace on his face. It was the last time he ever took the field without headgear.

"Sure," I said—my family's word. But it was a reflex. I knew he was talking about the kind of pain you see on the news and in movies, gunshot wounds.

"I mean *pain*," he said.

"I think so." Guys do this to each other, challenge each other, and you end up claiming that you know all about something you don't.

"I mean pain in your bones, Buchanan. *Bone* pain."

"I'm sorry about what happened," I said. But I wanted to know: was he loading the gun when it happened? Was he showing off how cool he was, holding a gun like an accessory, what the well-dressed man of today is wearing?

"It's not so bad," he said, after a moment of silence.

I was a little confused. Did he want pity, or did he want respect for being tough? Or was he just being truthful? I realized that while I knew Merriman well, I had never really had much of a conversation with him. I had almost never called him on the phone.

Even that time we changed a tire beside the freeway, our talk had been swear words and complaints about how you couldn't find anything in a new car, not even the manual in the glove compartment. Now, voice to voice, I knew what it must be like to be Merriman, scouts driving down from the University of Oregon to watch him play in his junior year, and now all of it gone.

"You're going to be a fine quarterback," he said.

I wasn't happy with the way the conversation went

after that. We talked to each other like strangers, nice people, but embarrassed to be on the same planet. I couldn't bring myself to tell him I found it very difficult to talk to my parents.

Afterward I sat there on the bed, wondering if Merriman must hate me. It would be the kind of envy that would wear off, but maybe it wouldn't. Maybe Merriman would have to use a cane the rest of his life, walk with a limp.

It's brave when you have to bear a burden, and one of my favorite kinds of nonfiction stories is about athletes who crash off cliffs in cars or wake up one morning in an iron lung, and they don't get back into the gym and run the marathon six months later. They stay handicapped and they inspire children. There's always a picture in this kind of book, the athlete as he is today, beaming from a wheelchair with smiling kids around him, or still blind, an open Braille book in his lap.

I admire handicapped people, but I wondered, sitting there on my bed, if that kind of story might be a kind of small lie, to make everyone feel better.

6

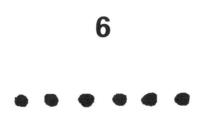

I debated whether to call Paula. But I knew I was going to call her before the inner argument even started. When I did, I was outside in the backyard. I had to be out in the fresh air when I talked to her. I was trying to break my Paula habit, and it was not that easy.

"Cray," she said when she heard my voice. She answered on the first half-second of ring, before anyone else in her house could move.

I started to tell her that there was some excitement at the factory today. I felt foolish, but I had this episode from real life, and I had played a part in it, and I just had to talk about it.

"I hated all the books I got out of the library today," Paula said, with that sexy little rasp in her voice.

Sometimes I hate Paula. She puts on one of these baby-talk lisps and says sexy things and I just about go crazy, getting stiff all over. I wanted someone like Kentia. Not *like*—I wanted Kentia herself, and it would be okay if she was not insane about the subject of sex morning, noon, and night. That would be the thrill, arm in arm with a woman you would turn to look at and think how cool and otherworldly she was.

I managed to get through the details of the fire and mentioned that some of the firefighters turned out to be women when they took off their helmets.

"Working around all those men," said Paula. *"Magnifique!"*

Paula could only think about the differences between men and women, and not just between the legs. If I said I had to go back into the house for my sunglasses, she would say, "Just like a man." I used to find this vaguely flattering, as though every time I popped a stick of gum into my mouth I was doing something macho.

"Brave boy," she said huskily, when I was done telling how I had been prepared to battle the fire with one portable fire extinguisher. *Brave boy*, in a little baby-talk voice.

The trouble was, it worked. She could peel me right off my good intentions like so much steam. "When are you coming over, Cray? I need you to rub my back."

"What time is it?" I found myself asking, before I could stop myself.

"I'm lying here on my tummy," she said. "I have a terrible crick in my neck."

She said *crick* like it was a code word for something tantalizingly obscene.

I reached the end of the long backyard, and looked out at the view. This was why we had bought the house, two years before. San Francisco glittered across the Bay. It wasn't just explosions I liked, devastation. I liked the stars, the tiny traffic.

"I'm nowhere near a clock," I said.

"You mean I have to move my body?" she said. She said that last word carefully, deliberately spacing it apart, *baw-dy.*

My dad had big plans for the backyard. A pile of gravel glowed in the light from the kitchen, next to a small mountain of sand. The gravel was gradually scattering outward, the peak growing shorter with the months, and neighborhood cats loved the sand.

Stakes and staves laid along the ground marked out where Dad was going to put in a sidewalk. Walking around back there, I was always tripping over a bag of cement or some of Dad's cement-working tools, the scabby hoe and the assortment of trowels, all of them getting rusty where the cement had blistered away.

She treated me to a moan as she rolled over and announced, "It's 10:05, Cray. And thirty seconds."

Paula once told me she could speak five languages. She could insult someone's mother in phrases from all over Europe. She knew Cantonese slang for *white person*, and knew the word for *whore* in languages I had never heard of. She could fire off delicious-sounding syllables and say, "That's Japanese for *Don't touch me there.*" I can say, "The red house behind the tree is very handsome," in Spanish, except I forget the word for *behind*.

"Tomorrow night," I said. I felt like telling her, "I am not having a conversation with you. You are talking. But I am watching an airplane glide overhead, red lights winking."

"Eight," she said. "Seven-thirty."

Strangers in Safeway see me, a tall, broad-shouldered kid, built like a lumberjack, and they smile. And I smile, too. And I mean the message smiles send out to people: I am nice, and you can trust me.

But sometimes in the back of the smile, behind the real niceness that fills up 98 percent of my mind, there is a small room with a gray creature in it, someone broadcasting nonstop, twenty-four hours a day, the Cray Buchanan World Service.

Detras and *atras.* They both mean *behind*.

I didn't think Paula had ever heard of either word.

As I was heading into the house I could hear him coming from a long way off, making his noise. I hadn't seen him for days, and I stood there marveling in an absentminded way that he was still alive.

7

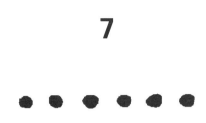

Anita had said we could not have him fixed because it wasn't natural, castrating a cat. He ran toward me through the dark, stiff-legged and crippled. I couldn't see him yet, but I could tell what he was doing, avoiding the chain-link fence along the hill, taking the long way around the blackberry hedge. He probably fell down once or twice. And he kept up his noise all the while, a very old and stubborn creature saying, "Ow, ow," over and over.

I felt sorry for Bronto, but I didn't like to pet him. He had little scars in his head where you usually scratch a cat. He couldn't even stand straight in the porch light, leaning into my pant leg, purring. I scratched him a little, with two fingers.

My dad was sitting with his head thrown back, his glasses crooked, his mouth agape like someone very old or very sick.

The television was on with the sound off. My

mother stared at it with her arms crossed in front of her chest. It was the usual TV mishmash, the Pope followed by an ad for denture cream. Big words jumped across the screen; people with the sound off weren't going to miss anything important.

"The beast is alive," I said.

My mother gave me a look: It meant either, You must be kidding, or, What on earth are you talking about?

I didn't call him Bronto in front of my mother because that was Anita's name for him. My mother called him Saucers. Five years ago, when the cat was a kitten, Mom had taught him to drink, nudging his face down into plates of milk. Anita said we should gave animals names that smacked of authority.

"He looks awful," I said.

Mom found a can opener beside the coffeemaker. She made a rattling noise with it, hitting it against the heel of her hand.

The cat door crashed, a paw found its way through the flap, and then the whole cat was inside. In the light he looked thin and moth-eaten, a bald place in his head next to one ear.

"Is he back again?" Mom said in a falsetto she uses only on cats. "Is he back again from being brave out in the world?" Talking to him directly. Mom found a can of Kitty Yummies in the back of a cupboard behind human food.

"When Kyle called earlier tonight," I said, "what did he want?"

"He wanted to speak to Anita," she said in her normal, flat voice.

"She'll be home soon," I said.

"She's late," said Mom.

I paused at the door to Anita's room and let the door swing slowly open. When Dad and Anita had one of their fights, it could be about anything. Once she had written the entire U.S. Senate, every single senator, about not cutting down the world's tallest sequoia, and she had used Ziff Furniture stationery, with the big green Z. She'd done it with a pen in longhand, no computer, so each senator would be impressed with the sincerity and effort.

Dad had been furious, and said that if she wasn't his daughter, he would have sued her for making the politicians believe Dad's business supported Anita's views. Actually, Dad didn't think the really historically important redwoods should be cut down, either. He just took a more complicated view of issues than Anita did.

Sometimes they argued about ordinary things, how the yogurt containers in her room would attract roaches. And at times like that Dad would say he didn't know what was going to happen to her when she found out what life was really like.

————

Bay laurels grow in the East Bay hills. They branch in the creek beds and smell like a spice cabinet—spreading, snaking trees with slender leaves. I had hiked up the trails with my mom a few times, and I always loved the way she would look out over the view when we reached a hilltop and tell me what was not there anymore.

"That used to be an inland sea," she would say. "All the way to the foothills. Saber-toothed tigers and dire wolves hunted these slopes, in what is basically contemporary time, maybe fifty thousand years ago."

I carried my mother's pack for her, and it gradually filled with rocks, Franciscan formation sandstone. Or maybe chert. Rocks the color of toasted bread the way I like it, light brown. I was there when she found it, chipping with her rock pick at the side of a cliff, breathing hard—this was before she lost all the weight.

I had it there in my room. I could look at it when I got tired of her report on the taxonomic features of an extinct species of bay tree. Paragraph after paragraph told how this was a kind of tree that had died out, and our current bay trees were a different variety—a new species.

The stone was sandwiched together, and as I sat on my bed, I opened the rock, and there it was, just as she had found it that day, so excited she jumped up and down. The fossil leaf was a stain in the rock, the size and color of a deer's eye.

Had Anita read the report all the way through? I wondered. Or had she started and quit right away? It was interesting up to a point, stem diameters, millimeters, and comparisons with bay trees in faraway places. But it was boring, too. Not boring and ridiculous, but dull the way the financial page is—important, but not to me.

There was something a little worrisome about it, too. I could not see any difference between the ancient, sixty-five-thousand-year-old specimen and the leaves we had in the kitchen cupboard, next to the instant coffee.

I wondered if Mother realized this: She might be wrong.

The bed jumped, scaring me a little. Bronto stood in the middle of the bed, and because he was so stiff, he anchored himself like a cat statue, giving me that cat hello, a gentle blink of the eyes. He was licking his whiskers. It was a little unusual for Bronto to come home at all, much less make his way into my room.

The form Coach Jack had given me was on the dresser, under a pile of paperbacks, the kind of novels I didn't like anymore, time travel and chopped-off heads. One edge of the release form was still curling from where Coach had rolled the paper up.

My eyes started to itch, and I looked in the mirror.

The whites of my eyes were pink, thanks to Bronto. I was starting to look like a boxer who was losing a bout, all puffy and flushed. In another few minutes I wouldn't be able to see. I fumbled through my top drawer.

My room was a museum, the way I used to be. I keep things. I care too much to give favorite toys to Goodwill. I don't keep everything, of course. But here was a beanbag monster, something from my early childhood, and here was a yo-yo that long ago had done tricks. Plastic space creatures, powerful, half-human figures—they were all there, in a great pileup with useful items, dead batteries and virgin batteries all mixed up together.

I wasn't even that interested in galaxies anymore, I just kept the space creatures for decoration. I found some Benadryl in the corner of the drawer, among the lint and yo-yo strings. The pills make me sleepy, but I'm allergic to cats, and the mirror showed me the face of a boxer who was going to be counted out, not because he was hurt, but because he was growing too ugly.

One of my favorite novels when I was younger was a story about a television reporter who hears a voice in his sleep. It is someone from another time, another reach of the universe, someone in trouble with his world. The powers of his time and place want him dead, and he can only escape by finding a person in a distant time to change places with him. And it happens: The drowsing man in Los Angeles wakes up in a landscape with scarlet skies and five moons.

But there is a conversation with this space fugitive, and I can't remember how it goes. I can't remember if the man in L.A. is convinced that he should come to the assistance of this dream voice, or if he is forced to change places whether he wants to or not.

I found one of Bronto's fleas on my ankle, right by the heel bone. When I dug a fingernail into the tiny insect, it broke in two, scrambling and going nowhere, leaking a little bit of my blood.

8

When I woke I sat up at once, thinking: What was that?

Bronto was gone, and there was a light on in the house somewhere. Someone had forgotten to turn it off, I told myself. I could forget about it and go back to sleep.

But the light was bright, a lance of it falling through the bedroom door. The door had opened somehow, and the light was getting brighter the longer I lay there. I would have to climb out of bed, go downstairs, and turn off the lamp. It was one of those simple problems that loom when you are still half-asleep and don't want to get up.

And then I heard my dad's voice. I knew he was on the phone by his tone, and the rhythm of his speech. He would talk, and then there would be a silence. Then his voice again, even more tense, and another silence. He was arguing with someone, keeping his temper. I could not hear the words.

It was one-fifteen. I tried to tell myself that this was one of those Dad problems, an issue that had nothing to do with me. Sometimes he stayed up late, calling Poland, where the bentwood chairs were made and shipped in pieces, spools and chair legs, to be assembled here. I heard my mother's voice, questioning.

I never have figured out what to wear to bed. I hate pajamas, largely because I always outgrow them so fast, and when they are tight not only do you look gawky, with your arms too long, but when you wake up with an early-morning erection it sticks out obviously and embarrassingly. Even when no one is looking, I don't like to feel awkward about what I'm wearing.

These days I tended to wear a large gray sweatshirt to bed, but I still had to pull on a pair of pants to make myself fit for company. Dragging on the pants made this all the more significant—there was something going on.

I padded down the stairs in my bare feet. The wooden steps were cold. The lights were on the living room, every single lamp, but there was no one there, only rumpled places in the chair and the sofa, impressions of their weight.

My dad had just put the telephone down, and he was looking at me without seeing me.

"What's happening?" I said.

"Dad was calling BART police," said Mom.

I didn't like the way that sounded, and a very bad

feeling flickered in my stomach. Then it was gone, and with a certain tenseness in my body I felt myself grow just a little stupid as a form of protection.

Bay Area Rapid Transit is a subway system. BART has its own police department. It is its own world— you buy a ticket and you enter transit land, scenery blurring by.

"The Oakland Police Department suggested it," said my mom, sounding overly calm, someone reading lines from a book. She didn't have to tell me. Anita wasn't home yet.

"It's only one o'clock," I said. "She's late." I meant: She's been late before. That wasn't quite true. She was rarely this late.

"That's right," she said, not looking at me. "She must have gone somewhere with Kyle."

Anita always called when she was even a few minutes late. Anita was impatient with the rest of us, but she played by a certain set of rules: Write letters, make phone calls, don't eat any more red meat than you have to.

I wondered if there had been an accident, one of the trains derailing. Sometimes someone jumps onto the tracks on purpose or by accident, the electric third rail cooking them stiff. These were my thoughts, but I heard my dad say, "The OPD says she hasn't been gone long enough for us to file a missing persons report. But they took her description anyway, because of her age."

"She's only running a little behind," Mom said, like someone referring to a train schedule. "God knows I was late all the time," she said, looking off to one side, like she could see herself twenty years ago. "I bet I took years off my dad's life," she said, without much sadness, but philosophically, puzzled by historical fact.

Anita worked near the MacArthur BART station. She would travel past the Nineteenth Street Station, Twelfth Street, Lake Merritt, and get off at Fruitvale. She would take the bus up into the hills. Dad had hated the plan, because of all the street crime, but she had found the job on her own and was even joining a union.

"Maybe she made some new friends," Mom was saying. "They stopped by after work."

Stopped by for a drink, she meant, or a cup of coffee. That didn't sound like Anita. The legal drinking age is twenty-one, although Anita could pass for older in bad light. Anita drank coffee a little, after dinner at a nice restaurant. But she made friends slowly, like me. Maybe she was changing. But this sounded like a fantasy that belonged to Mom's vision of the world, not Anita's.

Mom had friends, went out, drank caffe lattes in San Francisco. Anita was always in a hurry somewhere, running her fingers through her hair or giving it a toss to swing it out of her eyes.

"She was supposed be home at ten," Dad said. He

did not look sleepy, and he had combed his hair. He was dressed in slacks and a fresh shirt, but he was barefooted, like me.

"It's very inconsiderate," said Mom, not looking at either of us.

"What's the name of her manager?" Dad asked both of us. This was a word out of Dad's way of life: manager. If you needed help, you talked to the person in charge.

I gave him a look, a shake of my head: I don't know.

"I get an answering machine," said Dad. "I call American Shelf and Filing and I get a machine to talk to." He said this like it was an outrage he was bearing with as much patience he could muster.

"It's good they have an answering machine," I said. "The phone could just keep on ringing. You wouldn't like that." Maybe I was taking Anita's part, without thinking much about it. "Paula stays out to three sometimes." I said it like this—not *till* three. Maybe I was signaling to everyone by speaking a little clumsily that I didn't know what I was talking about.

My mother turned her head in my direction.

Paula had claimed to have stayed out with guys with motorcycles and Romanian accents, including one man years older than Paula who built sky-scrapers, driving rivets. His favorite expression was "Don't look down," in a foreign language I had never heard of.

50

"Last year I didn't get home until two-thirty that time," I said.

"I remember," said Mom, giving her words special weight.

"You both go to bed," Dad said.

Mom started to speak and he shook his head, and that was all anyone could say.

"I wasn't home until almost three o'clock that time," I said.

"You got on the phone," said Dad. "Oliver had a flat tire, and you called us twice, telling us you were okay." Merriman and I had gone to San Jose to see a hockey game, and it took us half an hour just to find the jack.

I had always wondered when Anita would do something like this. I had been expecting it in the back of my mind. Someday, I had come to believe, she would stay up all night and come home drunk. Or too happy, eyes bright with what Dad always referred to as Some Sort of Drug. As in: I think some of the people in the finishing room are on Some Sort of Drug.

She had gotten good grades, except in math, returned her library books on time, learned to drive in about half an hour one Saturday afternoon. She had been too good, in the way kids are said to be good kids. It was time. Anita had finally decided to have a wild night, and I couldn't really blame her.

But my parent's tenseness ate at me, even when I

went back up to my room. I wanted Anita to come home, say she was sorry, give a normal excuse, and then we could all go to bed, after Dad got over his speech about responsibilty, fumed a little, paced around for a while, and finally gave her a hug.

And I was afraid in a part of me that could not hear my own inner lecture. I lay down in the dark and tried to trust my parents to deal with this. I tried to trust Anita, too. She had kept her own address book since she was thirteen. Computers, Spanish verbs—it all came easily to her.

So I knew she would be all right.

9

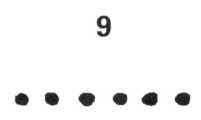

An engine started up outside, a beefy rumble.

It was still dark out. I got up in time to see Dad's white Jeep veer out of the driveway. Gears clanked. The two headlights illuminated the sprawling junipers in the front yard while Dad pumped the clutch, trying to shift. Our front yard was in good shape. A man from Green Planet Garden Service dropped by to touch it up once a week. Round stepping-stones led out into the middle of the lawn.

We have three cars, a twelve-cylinder Jaguar, a vintage MG, and the noisy Jeep. Each car is fun, and each has something wrong with it. We have money—a cabin at Tahoe, raw land on the north coast. But my dad's life is crammed with projects.

As Dad found first gear and accelerated, I caught a glimpse of his profile, portable telephone held to his ear. I could picture my dad following his plan, step by step. First, visit the place where Anita worked. There would be a night crew, security guards. Maybe Anita was still there, so involved in her work she couldn't turn her head to look at the clock.

\ Then he would cruise the BART station. After that he would follow the route home, checking out the bus stop, driving the short distance from the bus stop here, stopping every now and then to peer.

Sometimes when I came home late from football practice, he had been just getting into the Jeep, really annoyed, or standing at the curb with his hands on his hips. In some families I had the feeling you could vanish for most of the night and no one would ever ask. Around here we kept schedules.

I could hear the Jeep all the way down Lincoln, past Head-Royce School, the clutch slipping whenever Dad had to accelerate out of a full stop. It was a surprise to me he never got a ticket for having such a decrepit muffler.

I imagined seeing what he did as he drove: parked cars, empty streets. I imagined how Anita would look when the headlights caught her, marching, half-embarrassed to be so late.

I think I slept.

When I woke up I felt around for the clock, thinking I still had that old clock, Felix the Cat with clock hands on his face and an old-fashioned alarm bell. An alarm like that makes you wake up with your heart pounding, and that was how I felt now. No alarm had gone off. There was only silence. I kept the Felix the Cat clock in the bottom drawer. It was a joke between Anita and me, how scary cartoon figures would be if you saw them in real life.

I had not heard the Jeep come back, and I thought, now they are both lost somewhere.

But the white Jeep was parked in the driveway, swung hard to one side, engine off, headlights dark. So it was all right, I told myself.

Lamps were still bright downstairs. I was a little ashamed—I had made up my mind to stay awake, but I had missed the drama between Dad and Anita, Mom as referee.

I tugged on my pants again. My digital clock showed 4:15, and the clock is a little slow. Almost time to get up and go running. If I was going to play this fall, I would have to build my stamina.

But I had no intention of running. Football didn't matter to me now. I listened at my bedroom door. He was talking. He was down in the kitchen, and he was on the phone. I found myself down the stairs and in the kitchen before I was aware of taking any steps. Something about his tone brought me downstairs in a rush, and I waited for his words to make sense to me.

Mom sat, looking blank, in a chair that didn't belong in the kitchen, a gray wicker chair from my parent's bedroom. This out-of-place furniture bothered me, a sign of disorder. She had a big notebook open in her lap. I knew what it was, but I didn't like to think about why it was there.

The kitchen had a warm, yeasty smell, and the timer light, a little red dot, showed that dough was rising in the bread machine.

"She told us she was helping with inventory," Dad said into the phone.

It was one of those frustrating moments when I think my parents are out of their depth, like children.

Dad flicked his eyes at me, walking back and forth, wiping the sink with a sponge, wiping the kitchen table as he talked.

"She never worked that late," he said with a flat tone, repeating what someone was telling him.

The telephone made its faint squawking sound, and I tried to make the distant voice into words, a sentence, and I almost could: No, Anita had not been working until nine-thirty for the last week. Never later than seven or seven-thirty.

These were almost the exact words. I could tell by the pauses, the spurts of speech, translating them into a message that made me cold.

When Dad was off the phone, he sat down at the kitchen table, only to get up again and shift the sponge to its usual place, behind the faucet. "I went to the police," he said.

I didn't say anything.

"Just finding out what the procedure was," he said. It was like he could read my mind. He didn't look me in the eye, his voice quiet and steady. He was wearing the belt Anita had give him on Father's Day, just weeks before. It was an expensive glove-leather belt with a solid brass buckle.

"You talked to her manager?" I asked.

"I woke him up," he said. "I looked through my files. It turns out we both served on that Save the Bay panel a couple of years ago." Some businesspeople and some activists had joined together to tell the governor that the perch being caught in the South Bay were too toxic. My dad belonged to twenty different committees, heading most of them.

"She was always so smart," said Mom. She said this with a tone of admiration, nearly. She had that book of snapshots, a photo album, open in her lap. "When she comes home, I don't want you to yell, Derrick."

I knew how my mother's mind worked. Anita was seeing somebody. That was the way Mom would phrase it to herself. She would not say she was dating somebody none of us knew, or that she was having sex maybe even now, out there in the world.

I can't think like this. When I do, I put it out my mind—the thought of my sister being like other females in her private life.

"She can't do this," he said, but his voice was under

control. He meant she couldn't do to this to him, and to Mom. And maybe I was included, too, in his sense of quiet outrage.

He nodded after a moment, as though her words had finally hit him. He silently agreed—no yelling. But I also knew he was treating her absence as a rebellious act, something between Dad and daughter. We all knew that was the most hopeful way to look at it. But that wasn't why he had gone to the police station.

I visualized Anita in my mind seeing somebody. I thought of it like that: a man standing on a corner, a shadowy figure, Anita seeing him, running toward him, waving, in a hurry. A lover. It was romantic, out of a movie, autumn leaves and rainy streets.

An affair. I had seen those paperbacks in her book bag, behind the National Geographic videos and the hardbacks on veterinary science—half-naked aristocrats with muscles. They wrapped their arms around the governess, the young American visitor, the high school senior from Oakland.

"There weren't any reports," I said. I did not make it sound like a question. I meant: no reports of accidents. Car crashes. Or shootings. No rapes, no kidnappings.

"I even had them check the morgue," Dad said.

10

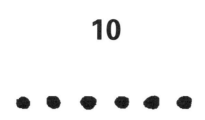

That proved it—he was quiet, to look at, but close to his own personal brand of hysteria. He had been down practically looking at all the people who had died since ten o'clock. My father was in a quiet panic, and Anita was going to clump through the door any second.

"You both go back to bed," Dad said.

"You went all the way down to the police station and asked about dead bodies?" I asked, double-checking, hoping that maybe he would laugh a little and admit that was going too far. My mind works like this sometimes, circling back like a sniffing dog.

"Sure."

The police headquarters in Oakland is miles away, almost to the Bay, a boxy, businesslike building. It was near a freeway, a double-decker highway that had partly collapsed in an earthquake. It was my father's favorite sort of neighborhood, warehouses and the kind of restaurant that specializes in quick lunches. I could imagine the police being very nice to him, not telling him that he was just another over-wrought parent. In a small way I was thankful that Dad had gone so far down his own mental checklist.

"What did they say?" I asked. I didn't like the way my voice sounded, years younger. It was also a painful question. What I really meant was, What could they do? And how many people had died that night? If we were all going to go crazy, let's do it to-gether, I thought. I found it reassuring, too. Anita was alive and well.

She was only a few hours late. I tried to deny it, but it was out of character for Anita to be away nearly all night. She would spring into the house, with some bright explanation.

Accidents and doctors didn't bother Anita, although she once said that everyone should be allowed to take a pain pill before they had a shot. She said her rare visits to Dr. Ames, the dentist, were calming, sit-ting there looking at the ceiling. One of the few times I had seen Anita really startled was when she nearly stepped on a gopher snake in the backyard, the brown-dappled creature whipping across the dirt and into the weeds.

Dad put his hand on my shoulder and gave it a squeeze. A good squeeze, like he was feeling the muscle, the bone. "I'm going to make some oat-meal," he said.

My mother didn't move. She wore the bathrobe

Anita had given her the Christmas before. We all called it the spinach-omelette robe, yellow-and-black plaid flannel. Mom had a silver-colored clip in her dark hair. Anita got her blond looks from Dad. I knew it had not been Mom's idea to get out all the old photos.

We all jumped a little when a grinding noise erupted from a corner of the sink. Mom had poured the ingredients into the machine before she went to bed, and now the bread maker was following the commands of its internal computer. I found myself wondering if it was making whole wheat or rye. Anita preferred whole wheat.

I hadn't wanted to tell my parents about the flat tire the year before, not in every detail. Merriman thought the tire had been slashed. Someone had stuck a blade into the sidewall, but not all the way through—just enough so that twenty miles up the freeway, the Michelin blew.

Merriman has dark skin, the color of strong coffee. He told me some people didn't like someone like him driving a brand-new Mercedes. I didn't see things that way—once a graffiti artist had covered Ziff Furniture with four-letter words. It isn't always racism or bigotry. Sometimes it's just mean fun.

It was as though I wanted to protect my parents from some ugliness in the world. Maybe I was embarrassed for people, knowing that my parents were

61

warmhearted and would not understand cruelty. I felt the same way about an especially bloody fight at school. I just didn't like to talk about it at home.

"You know what they kept asking?" Dad said.

I was supposed to bounce the conversational ball back, and I did. "What did they keep asking?"

"They kept asking if we had a fight of some kind."

I thought it was a pretty good question. But Anita and my dad had never had fights the way the Blankenships did, howled curses and the tinkling, crashing of God-knows-what getting smashed. Our family arguments had been only a little more heated than talk shows on Channel 9, pointed disagreements about whether chickens should be kept in cages or be allowed to range free.

"They keep suggesting maybe she's off with a friend," Dad was saying. "They say maybe she had some reason to be alone."

"Things like that happen." Where did I get this tone in my voice, this sound of reason and calm?

"Kyle knew," Mom said, looking straight at the wall.

Dad had a bottle of Windex out, and a roll of paper towels.

"Why else," she said, "would he call and ask to speak to her?"

Maybe she was with Kyle right now, I thought. Dad squirted Windex on the stove top. "I called Kyle," Dad said.

"You called Kyle's house?" I heard myself say.

Dad gave a quick nod, a silent *sure*.

That was even more dramatic than checking the list of unclaimed bodies with the police. I had to marvel at my father. When he went to battle stations, he went all the way. "You talked to Kyle's dad?"

Dad was wiping the top of the stove with the Windex, making it shine. "For a second or two."

Kyle's dad was the most unfriendly person I had ever met. He had made his money selling house trailers. I had never heard him speak a complete sentence. Kyle was tactless and curt, but his dad was like someone who would blow your head off. Plus, he had just had a pig valve put into his heart.

Mom tilted her head, meaning that she was listening but not about to talk. Dad was addressing her when he added, "Kyle says he doesn't know anything."

"I don't believe it," I said, and Mom gave a slow nod, her eyes closed.

I said, "Kyle knows."

"He was very sleepy," Dad said, as though that proved something.

"Kyle knows Anita wasn't telling us everything," I said. "All this time, shaving a few hours off work to—" To do what young women did with men. I was the one who would shout at Anita when she came home. "He knows who she's been going out with."

"Calm down," said my dad.

"I'm going to go get Kyle and drag him over here,"

I said. "I want him to sit right here in this kitchen and look me in the eye and tell me he doesn't know where Anita is."

"Relax, Cray," said my dad from somewhere behind me.

But I was rushing through the living room, hooking the keys to the Jeep off the plate on the side table with one hand, feeling my eagerness to have somewhere to go, something to do.

I could picture Kyle telling me he didn't know anything about Anita, his eyes looking everywhere but right into mine.

The sky was light blue to the east. A bird fluttered in the bottlebrush plant, chirping.

All night, I thought.

She's been up all night, gone, away. And she never called.

11

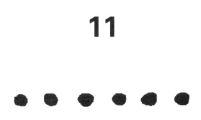

I flooded the engine.

I turned the ignition, pumped the gas, and the Jeep gave its hearty rumble, and then gasped. It choked and fell silent, rolling down the driveway a little by its own weight until I yanked on the parking brake.

Dad climbed into the silent Jeep and sat next to me. I could sense him trying to think of the right thing to say, looking away from me like a passenger enjoying the view—a front porch and an ornamental plum tree. The front garden had been planned by a man with an M.A. in gardening. He had started a company, Green Planet, and we were one of his first customers. No one else had stepping-stones leading up to their garden faucet, the step beside the dripping faucet green with moss.

"Why don't we have any normal cars?" I asked.

He rubbed his hands together like someone who was cold. It was gray but warm, low morning clouds overhead.

"You don't have time to do all the work," I said. I meant that I personally didn't know enough about cars to replace engine parts, clutch plates, whatever it was that had to be done. I couldn't help him—he would have to do all the under-the-hood labor himself. And I meant, what was going to happen today, a shipment of nightstands due out or we would never make the deadline.

"The Jeep is great off-road," he said.

We shifted into four-wheel drive about once a year, in the Sierra, near our cabin at Lake Tahoe. The Jeep could drive up and down cliffs, especially in reverse. But it was clear to me that my father liked his cars for reasons that had only a little to do with how they performed.

"Mom is picking out a picture of Anita," I said.

"Just in case they need one," he said.

I stared up the street, willing myself to see her. I closed my eyes. Count to three, I told myself, and open them—she'll be here.

We got out of the Jeep and went inside.

We sat in the kitchen, taking turns calling emergency rooms, starting with Kaiser Hospital and Summit, and working down the list. I was surprised how many hospitals there were. They all recognized my sister's description from my father's earlier call—long blond hair, gray-blue eyes.

Some of them were convalescent hospitals, nurs-

ing homes. I didn't call them. But I called every surgery center and twenty-four-hour clinic in Alameda
County. She began to sound like a character in a
story, Alice in Wonderland, someone pretty but
imaginary.

My dad had already called each hospital two or
three times, and by the time I was asking the question
the response was sympathetic but a little clipped, and
one nurse told me *she* would call *us* if there was any
word. But there was always a moment or two while
the receptionist checked a list, surveyed a list of
names, people who were brought in during the last
hour.

The entire house smelled like baking bread.

For a while, I decided to play a sort of game. The
game was: Pretend this is some other day, Anita in
bed asleep. I went about a normal routine and took a
shower, washing my hair with Breck's baby shampoo.
Anita had pointed out that it didn't leave gunky condi-
tioner in my hair, and it didn't make me have to squint
and grimace while I went about washing myself,
which is supposed to be a pleasant experience.

As soon as I turned off the water, I could tell nothing
had changed. The silence felt the same. I opened the
door of the bathroom, swirling steam slipping out
into the hall, and listened. Dad had a radio on in the
room he used as a den, where he kept his books and
videotapes. A radio voice talked about the morning

traffic, the Dumbarton Bridge closed westbound due to a big rig that had flipped.

I dried my hair in the doorway to Mom's room. I almost never walked all the way in. She sat at her desk, her head in her hands.

Her office is like the headquarters of a successful expedition. At her elbow, beside the computer printer, was the top section of a Neanderthal skull. It was just the bony bowl of the cranium and the brow ridges, the eye sockets only half there. I had always felt the wonder of having such a relic in the house.

Messages come in on the fax machine, by e-mail, questions from scientists in Boston, New York. My mother is an expert on the East Bay Hills. She is famous among ten people, and they all like to hear from her.

My mother was at her desk, the way she would be all morning on a usual day. But it was too early, and she was not working. I knocked gently on the door.

I couldn't tell if she heard me.

"Mother?"

She wasn't weeping. Weeping would be better than this. She sat looking straight ahead, at the computer, the row of rodent jaws. It struck me how little my family looks at each other. Eye to eye.

"You want me to help a little later?" I asked.

"Help," she said, saying the word like a foreign sound.

"Screen some sand?"

"I have about twenty pounds of it," she said. She turned her head so I could see her profile. She had lost the weight too fast, I thought. Her neck skin was slack. Fossil collectors in the field often collect bone-rich earth by the bucketful. Sometimes I shook dirt through a screen, picking out the tiny ribs and teeth that sifted free.

"I have to report to Jesse in the afternoon," I said.

We were doing really well. Like actors hired to play us in a movie, an early rehearsal, but none of us showing how scared we were. Our remarks didn't fit together very well, but that didn't matter. "Derrick won't be going in to work," she said.

Of course not, I thought.

"But you might as well," she said.

My family had a rule about taking time off from school or work: you never did. Unless you were paralyzed or had major surgery. The Monday I spent home with my concussion, seeing double, was the first day I had spent home since eighth grade. I had been sick sometimes during those years, but I went to school with a fever more than once, and one spring I had poison oak so bad the school nurse sent me home.

Dad never took time off. Not when he worked as a furniture designer in San Francisco, sixteen hours a day, planning a revolution in wicker. He won awards, made money, bought a factory, and now he could work every hour of the day if he wanted to.

Mom picked a blue notebook off her desktop, and held it up by her ear. "Take this down to Derrick," she said.

I didn't want to take it, but I did, and I didn't stop to glance into Anita's room when I passed the door.

12

● ● ● ● ● ●

Dad was standing in the front doorway, full daylight through the open door, morning clouds burned away.

"You better go talk to Mom," I said.

He turned, looked me a question, and I handed him Anita's blue address book.

He opened it very carefully. It was a new book, the most recent in Anita's long history of phone numbers. The pages turned stiffly. Anita had very correct printing, made for keeping records, filling out forms. She knew a lot of people.

Even upside down I could make out familiar names, Kyle Anderson right at the beginning of the book. One summer, when I was nine, Anita had pretended she was a librarian. She made library cards for each of us, and kept records, checking out old *Scientific Americans* to Dad.

"Look through here and see if—" He couldn't complete the thought. He wanted me to see if there was a name I didn't recognize, or a name I did, someone dangerous, mysteriously attractive.

"We shouldn't be looking at her stuff," I said.

"Who is this?" said Dad, showing me a name, Dr. Coors, with an address on Piedmont Avenue. I turned the pages of the address book, hearing Anita's exasperated whisper in my mind. When she was annoyed she dropped her voice to a hiss. She didn't like to shout. She would understand when she saw how tired we looked. We didn't know what else to do.

"Who is Dr. Coors?" asked Dad, demanding. He wanted Dr. Coors to be the name we were looking for, a shadowy doctor, specializing in street drugs.

Dr. Coors had very blond, nearly white, curly hair up and down his arms. "He gave Bronto his shots," I said.

Dad took the stairs three at a time, hurrying to talk to Mom. I followed more slowly and stopped at Anita's room.

Mother had been everywhere, tugging drawers, opening files. Boxes were open, old videos and comic books, remains of Anita's childhood, scattered across the floor. Mom was good at this sort of thing. Even the mess was more organized than it looked, her old jump ropes in a pile with her obsolete, worn-out Ping-Pong paddles and brightly colored tennis balls.

A diary was open beside a stack of old report cards.

Mother had no right to look at this, and there it was, spread open in the morning sun.

I sat on the bed. Anita's graduation picture was on a far shelf. It didn't really look like her. There was a school district rule for those photos—everyone had to wear the same sweater, a similar pearl necklace. I was going to have my own graduation portrait snapped in a few weeks, a jacket and tie, "preferably a dark tie and a gray-to-dark jacket, navy blue allowable."

I don't know who sets this kind of policy. But the result is that graduates, photographed almost a full year before, look a little bit like strangers, people smiling while they hold their breath. Here was this richly colored portrait of Anita, her chin down, her eyes steady, the mandatory smile. She had worn jeans to the photographer's, and paint-spattered tennis shoes without laces, well-dressed only from the waist up.

When the pictures came in the mail, in those stiff cardboard, do-not-bend envelopes, she had threatened to burn them. As a joke. I think she liked the one we all picked out. And I wondered if this is how Anita might look to a stranger, a lecher in a passing car, someone who didn't even know her name.

Every time I looked at the clock, I could not believe how slowly time passed.

When the phone rang, someone snatched it eagerly, but it was always only Anita's boss or Jesse, re-assuring Dad but having to call him four times be-tween six-thirty and eight forty-five to get straight on what had to be done with the hopper, when the fire in-spector was coming.

"Until she comes home," my dad said, concluding each phone call. He's almost the only person I know who doesn't say good-bye when he hangs up. He ends phone calls like someone in a movie, just drop-ping the receiver.

"Kyle is coming by," said Dad after another phone call.

"Kyle is coming to tell us what he knows," I said. "He changed his mind. Decided to be helpful." I had changed my mind about wanting to see Kyle. I didn't want to see him, and I did not want Kyle here. My family was wounded, tired, and I didn't want to see Kyle's hard little eyes.

Kyle was probably stopping by to amuse himself. His own life was too boring. I knew we had always seemed colorful to him, everyone always in a rush. Nobody hurried in Kyle's family.

"He just said he wanted to share the worry," said Dad. "He'll be by as soon as he drives his dad back from an appointment with his doctor."

"I don't want to see him," I said.

Dad didn't seem to hear me. He paged through the address book. He had called several people, interrupting breakfasts, finding that people had already left for work. It was harder than calling hospitals.

Usually the person he called knew who my dad was, but he didn't know them, so there was a friendly, cheerful aspect to the call, talk about the weather, the lack of rain. What made it worse, my dad said more than once, laughing too energetically into the phone, was that all this worry might be totally unnecessary. She might be home any second.

I had a bad thought, revolving around the words you hear in the news, "beyond recognition." Maybe she had been in a fire, and her body had burned so badly it didn't look like her.

So I tried to have some other mental pictures— Anita on a ferry on the Bay, empty champagne glass in her hand. Anita sleeping off a wild party, inno- cently, curled up on a sofa, no head for alcohol. Anita waking and this very moment fumbling in her purse, finding coins, making the phone call.

Breathless, full of apologies.

We had all forgotten it. Only I remembered, and set the baked bread on the sink. It was honey brown, and still a little warm when I cupped my hands around it and really felt what was there.

When there was a knock at the front door, I knew it was Anita, too embarrassed to pop right in, too guilty to run all the way upstairs to pee or take off some

75

clothes that she couldn't stand anymore, too tight, too hot.

It was a woman I didn't recognize, and a car parked at the curb, one of those light green, almost colorless sedans. She gave me a card like a salesperson, a business card imprinted with the familiar oak-tree silhouette. But she didn't work for the school district. I gave the card a good look but still had trouble reading the words. I didn't have to; I knew what she was.

I thought that maybe this is how the news might come. If something terrible happened. If they found her, and the news was not good. The woman in a dark blue skirt and matching jacket asked to speak with Mr. or Mrs. Buchanan.

I let her in.

13

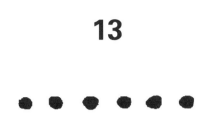

A man in a suit stepped in behind her, smelling of coffee and aftershave.

Her card gave her name as Detective DeAnne Waterman, from the Juvenile Division of the Oakland Police. Detective Waterman had long hair pulled back into a soft bun at the back of her head. There were two white streaks in her hair, the sort of lightning strikes some women have added in the beauty parlor.

The detective did not make any remark to me beyond asking to speak to my parents. I invited her to sit down, and she did, but on one of the blue wicker chairs people rarely used. She had a briefcase under her arm, a black bag with a shoulder strap. Her eyes were kind, dark, and I tried to read her mind by looking into them. She wasn't talking, but she was thinking, giving me a reassuring smile.

She waited to speak to my parents, and the man who was with her sat in my dad's favorite easy chair, leaning forward. He was quiet the way a Seeing Eye dog is, an important shadow. He had tiny pockmarks all over his cheeks. Both visitors were on edge, like they were going to start a footrace right there in the living room.

"Nice plants," said the man with the pinholes all over his face.

"I really admire someone with a green thumb," said Detective Waterman, both cops ready to play a game of Small Talk. She asked me my name and I told her. "The plants belong to my mother," I said as I went to get Dad.

My dad had heard them come in. He hurried to finish a phone call, and as soon as he hung up, he looked at my feet, afraid to catch my expression. "What did they say?"

I wanted to tell them all that it was too early to have the police sitting around in the dining room. I wanted to tell them everything he had done up to now was way too fast.

We all needed to slow down. I had the feeling we could punch a rewind button or pull the plug on the machine that made all the clocks run forward. Anita would be here, with something she had found, an old license plate she thought Dad would like, or a lizard skin, like the one she found last summer, like a plastic cutout with four legs.

I wanted to say all this, but all I said was, "They just want you and Mom." I couldn't bring myself to make another sound. This might be it, I knew. This might be the news my mother and dad had been afraid of since Anita was born. It was the news I was afraid of whenever my dad was late coming home, whenever my mom's plane was delayed.

I also wanted to add that they were both calm, nice. *Nice* is an important word. I like quiet, soft-voiced people. I did not feel they were here with bad news, but I could not be sure. Maybe they had especially pleasant cops deliver very bad news.

Dad left me, hurrying into the living room. One of the strands of my mother's coffee plant draped over Detective Waterman's shoulder.

"There's no news about your daughter," said Detective Waterman, a tiny drop of water from the leaves soaking into her jacket.

My mother appeared at the top of the stairs. "There's no news," my father repeated, to my mother, to all of us. It was almost wonderful—no bad news. And then the tiredness came back all over again.

My mother had put on a dress she never wore, something with a sash, a sea green cloth that looked all wrong this time of day. No one can change her appearance as dramatically as my mother. Most of the time she looks like a frumpy ranch hand, someone who could shoot a buffalo in her spinach-omelette bathrobe. Now she looked like a weary hostess. She extended her hand and thanked them for coming over, like they were new neighbors.

"Missing Persons and Juvenile work hand in hand," said Detective Waterman. "On weekends we work out of the same office." She said this just as she took my mother's hand, as if the two of them were acting out a skit, "The Inner Workings of the Oakland Police."

It was not a weekend, I wanted to say. It was Friday.

They all followed my father into his den. There was a table over to one side, covered with photos of Anita.

My dad's den is a room of shelves and books, a television only he watches, a small Sony perched on a pile of old magazines. The wall is decorated with maps of faraway islands, atolls, and reefs.

I didn't like the man with the pinprick holes in his face. He looked at me from over by the maple accent table, an item Ziff used to make until earlier that year. The cop looked at me again after a few moments, keeping his finger on a picture of Anita on her seventeenth birthday. She was wearing a sweatshirt and cutoff Levi's. I had been in charge of the camera that day. The picture was a little blurred, the camera strap a fuzzy gray caterpillar at one corner of the photo.

I couldn't stop myself from having this thought: I could match myself against this man physically and win. He was muscled under his poly-blend suit jacket and probably knew some police academy choke holds. But if I put a shoulder into him, he would go down.

Right in the middle of this thought, the cop gave me a smile. The little holes in his face closed up when he showed his teeth, his eyes warm, and I felt how mistaken I was. I felt how jagged I was inside, shaky, nothing fitting together. Detective Waterman glanced my way and she smiled, too. She was pretty in a no-nonsense way. It bothered me, how badly my mood matched what was really happening, two police here to help my family.

"I took a lot of those pictures," I said.

I was ashamed at the quality of the photos. I can take a good picture, with a little luck. My camera work was betraying Anita, making her look like someone she wasn't. I imagined Detective Waterman going around to motels with one of my snapshots. Did you see anyone who looked like this? she would ask. And the motel clerk would say no, even though Anita was sleeping in room 9 that very minute.

"What do *you* think?" asked Detective Waterman, looking right at me. I tried to imagine her with her hair wet down to her shoulders, telling her hairdresser, "I want lightning bolts, one on either side of my head."

"Can you think of a reason Anita didn't come home last night?"

I shook my head, the way someone does at supper when his mouth is full and he can't answer right away. But it was feeling that kept me from talking for a moment. Detective Waterman clicked her pen, a gold ballpoint

"I think she's all right," I said. My voice was ragged. "I think she's with someone."

"Do you think," asked Detective Waterman, "maybe she decided to leave—and not come back?"

"She needed a life of her own," said my mother, like someone reading the title of a story in a magazine. The pain in her voice hurt me.

Some routine places should be checked, my dad said. The land up in Mendocino, the cabin at Tahoe. A local park ranger or sheriff could pay a visit to those places, my dad was saying, trying to calm us down by sounding in control. Detective Waterman made a note and said, "I'll follow up on that."

"She left a new pair of pants," I said. "Folded on the chair."

I had their attention. They needed me to complete my thought. I said, "She'll be here any minute."

It was natural for Kyle to make his entrance then. He knocked, but the front door had been left open, and his knock was a faraway noise that didn't catch anyone's attention.

His voice reached us from somewhere in the living room, all the way inside the house. "Hello?"

My dad looked up sharply and my mother didn't seem to hear a sound. Dad made a motion with his head, meaning, Go see what he wants.

I closed the door to the den firmly behind me. As I left I heard Detective Waterman ask how much Anita weighed.

———

I greeted Kyle and told him there wasn't any news. I asked if he would like to sit down, and he sat.

"It's ten-thirty," he said.

I wanted to argue that it wasn't that late in the morning, but the antique clock in the corner agreed with Kyle.

I hadn't eaten anything since last night's lasagna. "Would you like some toast?" I asked.

"No," said Kyle.

"How about some orange juice?" I suggested.

"No."

"I can warm up a Pop-Tart," I said.

"I ate," said Kyle.

Sometimes I would play a private game, offer him cold drinks, hot drinks, snacks, waiting for him to say "No, thank you." He would just get a certain stiffness to his head and shoulders, resenting each offer a little more. If I happened to mention something he would like, he never said "please." It was always, "I'll have some of that."

"I'm going to make myself some toast," I said.

"Something must have happened to her," said Kyle.

14

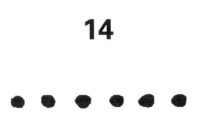

I asked him what he knew, who Anita's new boyfriend was, and his eyes just got smaller than they already were. Kyle looks like a handsome enough guy who has lived his whole life in a tunnel underground. I knew what Anita saw in him, a project, someone to make strong and healthy. She believed in animal rights, and Kyle was a kind of animal.

"I can't help you," said Kyle.

Maybe if your dad is a silent, mean person you never learn to use sentences. Kyle took calculus and had a watch with a beeper that was always going off at odd times, to remind him of duties he never explained. He talked like someone with his jaw wired.

"Anita has a lot of energy," I said. I meant: sexual energy as well as all the other kinds.

Kyle nodded, once, a quick up-down of the chin.

"There had to be some other guy," I said. I wanted to point out that Anita was a young woman with plans. Kyle, with his heroin-addict looks, was hardly going to please Anita when she found out how smart she really was.

That was the key to her: how much she could do with her mind, and how the rest of us must have seemed so slow to her, a family of sleepy, halting bears. I could see it sometimes, how much effort it took for her to be patient when I didn't understand how the famous gene scientist Mendel got white sweet pea blossoms to flutter on the vine next to the red ones.

And I'm not stupid. Spanish slows me down to a crawl, but I manage to take all university prep classes and avoid disaster. But I could see Kyle not really understanding what had happened, gazing around out of his tactless head, looking like a little boy grown tall overnight.

Maybe Kyle was a little afraid of me. He looked at me sideways. "I don't think there was anyone else, Cray. That's my honest opinion." He wanted to shut up, having trouble judging my mood. But he added, "I would tell you. Even if it hurt my pride."

I just couldn't work up any anger over him. I felt sorry for him. I could see that he didn't know anything. I had been hoping—depending on it. Now I felt dry all the way through.

"If you think of anything? . . ." I said, not finishing the thought, feeling for the first time in my life an awkward companionship with Kyle.

———

I was glad to get on the bus heading down Fruitvale. The day looked garishly normal, people driving, people standing patiently, waiting for the AC Transit bus to roll to a complete stop before they took a move toward it. Even the high-crime areas, windows behind black grills, were sunny, mail being delivered, people carrying groceries.

I was useless around the house, Dad on the phone, and Mom circling him like a major planet, feeding him phone numbers, hints. The police came and went, and I had Detective Waterman's card in my wallet. Every second I spent away from the house was a moment in which there could be good news.

If I stayed away, things could happen. Anita could come home, tell her story, and life could go on. It was like waiting for something wonderful, Christmas, that trip to Yellowstone when I was nine. If you think about it, the hoped-for joy stays away, and never comes any closer.

But I thought Barbara might brighten and give me good news as I rushed through the door into the office. She peered at me, a pile of invoices in front of her. She gave me a shake of her head: no news.

Jesse is as tall as I am. But he is broader chested, heavier all over. I found him in the cabinet room. Workers wielded staplers, hissing, banging. As usual, it was too loud to talk.

"Any news?" Jesse asked. He had to shout.

Jesse shows a feeling in his face as soon as he has it, amusement, irritation. I saw him fire someone for coming ten minutes late and the man didn't even argue, just turned right around and went home. "Not yet," I said.

Jesse winced.

"You want me packing drawer pulls?" I asked, shouting over the shriek of one of the wood-shaping lathes behind me. The machines take posts of wood, knotted and rough-cut, and shape them into bedposts or table legs.

"We're way behind," said Jesse, like this was what I wanted to hear.

Maybe it was. I love to catch up, pushing myself. Packing drawer pulls was fun without being something you would pay to do, and it was something that had to get done.

Each nightstand was shipped with a plastic bag in the drawer. Inside the plastic bag was a brass drawer pull and enough screws to put the handle in place. I stood beside a hill of slithery plastic bags and a box of screws. Behind me was a huge, bulging carton of drawer pulls, manufactured in Korea.

I counted out four screws carefully at first, popped them into a bag, dropped a brass handle in on top, and plunked the little package onto a conveyor belt. I couldn't see what happened beyond the pile of stacked, flattened cartons, but I knew that workers in the shipping room were putting the plastic bags of hardware into nightstand drawers and taping them to the bottom of the drawer so they wouldn't rattle around.

There were larger questions I could ask about all of this. I wanted to know why we couldn't ship the stands with the hardware already attached. I wanted to know how far behind the factory was running, and if we would make the deadline. I wanted to know if the fire inspector had arrived that morning, and what we were going to do to keep another fire from starting.

But I let myself not think. After a while I didn't have to count out the screws—I could pinch out four every time, without looking. The conveyor belt was a worn rubberized length with a seam that showed up periodically, a white scar in the dark gray, humming surface. Seeing it come around every fifty-five seconds was satisfying, hypnotic. It was one more thing that almost made me forget.

When my father bought the factory from Mr. Ziff, he said he would keep the name Ziff Furniture because it was so well known. Plus, he said, it didn't sound like a real name, but a name someone might make up, like the names for laundry soap—*Bold, Dash. Ziff*, Anita agreed, sounded like a sound effect in a comic strip, an arrow hitting its target.

Within a few weeks of owning the factory there was a very troubling accident. Dad would talk about it sometimes, but only when he was in the right mood.

Dad was in the office, trying to help Barbara boot up a new computer program, when Henry Wills ran up to the counter. He was breathing hard, his hand wrapped up in one of the pink shop towels. This shop towel wasn't pink anymore; it was red. Henry said he cut himself, and Dad asked him how bad it was. Dad doesn't like to describe what happened next unless he is sure the story won't upset his listeners.

Dad had trouble finding it. And when he did locate it at last, on a dune of sawdust, it didn't look like a thumb, already too white, too withered to be a human body part.

Dad hurried the thumb out to Jesse's waiting car, and Mr. Wills and the thumb arrived at the clinic. The thumb was reattached by Dr. Pollock, the surgeon, and when Mr. Wills retired the following year, he was walking around with five fingers just like everybody else.

As I worked on the bags of drawer pulls, I kept expecting a tug at my sleeve. I kept expecting Dad to be there, telling me in a tone of relief what had happened to Anita. He would be talking nonstop, why she couldn't get to a phone, telling me our lives could go on.

15

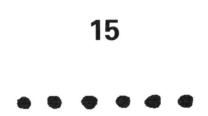

A buzzer sounded through the factory every working day at five o'clock. It was a bronze bray that cut through the rumble and hiss of equipment. There was a mix of people in the factory, men and women, people from faraway countries working alongside people who had lived in East Oakland all their lives. The closing buzzer changed the feeling in the air, and most sections of the factory fell silent, making the voices speaking Spanish and Cantonese suddenly sound loud.

The doors to the outside were wooden sections that slid sideways on rollers. I slipped out the shipping room door and ran along the outside of the factory as a shortcut. I was heading against the flow of workers at the front entrance. Most of them must have heard about my sister. The cries of "How's it going, Cray" and "Take care, Cray" sounded quieter than usual, concerned.

I knew that my father would be there in the office,

ordering paint or shop gloves, or meeting with the fire inspector. Dad would be there, and everything would be all right.

Jesse was there in Dad's place, his arms folded, nodding in agreement with a man in a dark zipper jacket and a clipboard.

"This is Cray Buchanan," said Jesse. He said *Cray* with special emphasis, giving the message that I was the owner's son without coming out and saying it. I caught the glint of a badge on the front of the zipper jacket, FIRE MARSHAL. I was suddenly tense. I had expected an ordinary inspector, someone with a list to check off. This man had the look of someone who could arrest us if he didn't like our answers.

I shook the marshal's hand, and I could sense his hesitation, wondering how seriously to talk to someone my age. "I'll report to my dad," I said. "Anything you have to say." But I didn't sound like a kid needing his father's backup. I sounded like someone who could think for himself, someone this man could talk to.

"I cleaned out all the ducts," said Jesse. "I had a crew on the roof all day, clearing all the sawdust. And fixing the hole the fire department chopped into the hopper." Jesse smiled. "So everything's okay."

Jesse was doing just a little bit of a selling job. Everything *was* okay, probably, but it was important that the inspector think so, too. The marshal had a mustache with a few glints of gray, and narrow eyes.

The eyes took in Jesse and switched over to me. It was impossible to tell what the man was thinking. He had one of those perfect faces for making people nervous—lean, showing little emotion.

"Let's go up on the roof," I suggested.

I was surprised when the fire marshal said simply, "I believe you." He patted his clipboard against his pant leg. "You don't want this place to burn down any more than I do."

"But you ought to go up and make sure," I protested. "Some of those sawdust fires start up again."

The fire marshal smiled a small, tough smile, one wrinkle in his cheek. He shook his head. "I'll schedule another inspection in about three, four months." We were due to have our fire extinguishers inspected then anyway, so he was basically telling us that nothing special was going to happen. It was like passing a test too easily. I wanted to argue with him, but I felt Jesse's big hand on my arm.

"Drop by any time you want," I said, sounding just as fake and easygoing as any grown man talking to an official who could shut down the factory and put it out of business. I had heard Dad sounding like this, as though his favorite moments were when the fire department came by to make sure the Dumpsters were emptied once a week.

"You employ how many people here—one hundred and ten, one hundred and twenty," said the marshal. He wasn't asking as much as thinking out loud.

"A little more," said Jesse.

"So if this place shuts down, it takes a big bite out of the economy," said the marshal.

I did something else I had seen experienced men do, and I felt completely phony doing it. I pointed my finger at him, with my thumb up, a silent way of saying "You're right."

The truth is that these little phony gestures and phrases work. You say them and people respond. The marshal gave me his card, the second card I had taken that day.

When the marshal was gone, I walked with Jesse out into the cabinet room. The place was silent, just one worker pushing a broom around, making a small pile of bent staples. The staples made a faint, tinkling noise along the concrete floor.

I had heard about factory owners paying bribes. Dad wouldn't do it, and Jesse wouldn't—at least, as far as I knew. But I suddenly wasn't so sure.

"I think he must have heard about your sister," said Jesse. "Decided to take it easy."

"He still should have gone up the ladder and made sure everything was safe," I said.

"He was giving us a break," said Jesse.

"What kind of a world is this?" I asked, too loudly. "People just go through the motions."

"You want me to run up the street and grab him?" said Jesse. "Tell him to come on back, we want to take him up on the roof whether he wants to take a look or not? I bet the two of us could drag him up there without much trouble." He was joking, but there was an edge to his voice.

The shipping room was the only department working overtime. The sound of a truck reached us, backing up to the shipping room door. Another shipment of nightstands would be in Southern California by midnight.

"I just think everyone needs to be more careful," I said. "Everyone has to do their job exactly right." My voice had taken on a thick, heavy sound, the way it does when I am saying one thing and meaning something else.

I could have called home from the office, sitting at my dad's desk. I thought about it, looking down at the clutter of business cards and memos all over my dad's work space. My dad had a collection of paperweights, rocks Anita had found on the beach. He needed them. His desk top was like his life, dozens of things to get done. One of the rocks had a barnacle on it, a chalk-white miniature volcano.

I actually had my hand on the telephone but I couldn't bring myself to use it.

"You be careful now," said Barbara as I left the office. She was one of those people who like to add an extra word or two to what they say, not "Good night," but "Good night now."

I turned to give her a wave, and the look she gave me made me stop. I pushed my way back through the swinging half-door at the counter. I could not keep myself from thinking: She knows something.

She knows something, and she doesn't want to tell me.

"No, hon, I haven't heard anything," she said, reading the question in my eyes.

She didn't seem to have a life outside the billing department. A row of framed pictures was on display on her desk, and I realized I had never really paid much attention to them. Children, I guessed. The two elderly people must be her parents. She got to work before anyone in the morning and worked long after the rest of us had gone, recording payments, billing furniture stores, sitting there gazing at numbers on the computer screen, pushing the delete button.

"Did Jesse really have a crew on the roof today?" I asked. I was stalling. I didn't want to go home. I knew what was happening, and as long as I stayed away I could pretend I wasn't a part of it.

Sometimes I walk down a street and I am surprised how easy it is to make a telephone call. Telephones are everywhere. The phone companies must think we can't go three minutes without talking to someone. You can carry a phone in your pocket just in case you need to hear a voice. There was a pay phone by the bus stop, a large metal frame shaped like a telephone receiver. But I didn't use it. The longer I went without knowing, the more time there would be for something to happen.

I didn't even let myself think her name. I didn't even let myself picture her face clearly in my mind, I thought of it with deliberate vagueness—by the time I get home, there will be good news.

16

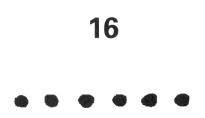

The Blankenships had been the first house on our street to order crushed white gravel. A small mountain of it had occupied their driveway for a couple of weeks. It wasn't simply white—it sparkled. The crushed quartz was spread by Mr. Blankenship himself, forming a bright white path that circled his lawn. Other neighbors decided that white gravel was a brilliant idea, and in the following months more dump trucks of glittering rock rolled up our street.

Now the Blankenships' gravel was scattering, bare places in the path. A strange type of weed grew in the midst of the gravel, a flat, spreading plant, looking like great green cow pies against the dazzling white. And the gravel found its way far from where it was supposed to be. I kicked a piece of gravel ahead of me, one great kick sending it all the way down the street. The closer I came to my house, the harder my pulse beat.

As soon as I saw my own house, I knew. I went sick-cold.

A blue van was angled up the driveway, right behind the Jeep. The van had KTVU all over it, big white letters, on the sides, on the back. Dad knows a few television people, serving on committees with TV- and radio-station owners. I could imagine him on the telephone, convincing one of his friends that this was a hot story.

But now I couldn't argue with the feeling I had. Dad was right. I stood in the living room, near the coffee plant, trying to hear what was going on in my dad's den. Whatever was happening, it was almost over. A pretty Asian woman with a startling amount of makeup came out of the den smiling, reaching for a briefcase a man was carrying.

I had seen this woman on television, and was surprised how young she looked, young and brightly colored, her face full of pinks of various shades, her eyes carefully outlined. She was wearing a dark blue jacket, and I remember thinking how amazingly pretty she looked, only a few years older than myself. Not sexy and not beautiful—someone you wanted to look at and never stop.

She had an assistant, a man who could have been the fire marshal's brother, one of those hard-looking men with steady eyes. The cameraman had baggy pants with about nine extra pockets and a blue T-shirt with MICHIGAN across the chest, yellow lettering. The

T-shirt had shrunk with use, and his arms stuck down from the shortened sleeves. He swung the tiny video cam from a strap.

I tried to judge from what was being said—and not said—what had happened.

Dad saw me but did not give me any sign except for an open-eyed expression I knew was supposed to communicate something. He walked his visitors down the front steps. He was talking about property tax. He said a special assessment had paid for the sidewalks in this part of Oakland. I did not mistake this patter for anything but filler talk, the chatter Dad keeps up because he can't keep quiet. He worked the talk around to streetlights, and then to crime, what he had been talking about all along even when he changed the subject a little, working around to the only thing that was really on his mind.

Mom came to my room. I had fled there. That was the only word for it. I saw these television people, their easy, relaxed faces, walking off with a news story about my sister, and I could not stand to talk to anyone.

I didn't mean to hide from the world. Sometimes, just like my mother, I need a few minutes to myself.

She sat next to me on the bed. She put her two hands together, her right hand over her left, so the wedding ring showed through her fingers as she massaged her knuckles, her fingers, taking some time out from talking. Dad's voice reached us from downstairs, his words muffled but his tone carrying through the floor from wherever he was in the house, portable phone to his ear.

"I can't look at it," Mom said at last. She was wearing a lab smock, a white coat. The pockets made a crumpling sound, a noise I recognized, typical of my mother under stress.

She put a small book into my hands, Anita's diary. It fell open to the same page I had seen the day before. The handwriting in her diary was so hurried, or so cramped with feeling, that I could almost convince myself it was not hers. But it was. The bottom half of one page was a single word, "Blisters," written in tall, scraggly letters. And beneath it, five exclamation points. She had bought a new pair of shoes for hiking and the right shoe had tortured her. A few nights ago she had sat watching television, putting Band-Aids on bright pink sores on her foot, the room smelling of disinfectant.

"Please," she said. "Please read it and tell me."

"The handwriting is a little messy," I said.

She gave a quick little nod. That was what we would both pretend—that Mom had trouble figuring out Anita's penmanship.

"There wasn't any news," I said, not asking, making it sound like an announcement.

"No," she said. "No news."

I really hated the posters on the walls, supernovas

and interstellar gas, the kind that glows purple by the time the sight of it reaches Earth. I had no interest in any of it. In another year I would be out of high school, and I had no plans. It struck me as I sat there with my mother weeping. She was trying not to, making the bed tremble. I would have to decide what college I would go to. And what I would major in—I would have to think about that, too. Not right away—not today, not this week.

But I was letting weeks slip by without thinking that I had a future. I sat beside my mother and read Anita's diary, from the first, neatly printed entries from almost a year ago to the bounding, energetic writing of the night I had seen her tending one of her blisters.

Anita indicated a break in time with a row of dots, small circles, six of them. Never five or seven. Six tidy circles that meant she had not written anything for a while. Sometimes a week had gone by, sometimes three. The time skipped was indicated by the same set of symbols, six dots.

I still thought that Anita might bound up the stairs, but I no longer felt I had to have an explanation ready. I could take as long as I wanted, turning the pages beside my mother, who fell still and silent. I trusted her quiet more than my father's chatter.

If an archaeologist discovered this journal centuries from now, brushed away the dust, and translated the scribbles, he would conclude that it was written by a young woman with no other human beings in her life.

There was no mention of any of us. Kyle's name appeared once—"Kyle thinks so, too."

It was a book of lists, mostly. Books she had read, books she wanted to read, movies she liked, movies she hated. Then the lists grew complicated, branching into arguments, why one author should not have killed herself, why she dreamed she was trapped in a movie about a recluse who found a human tooth in a hole in the wall of his dining room.

The summer before, Anita had begun reading biographies. She read about women who wrote books and poems, women who painted, sang the blues, ruled empires. She began to read diaries, the journals of famous people, writers who would start an entry, "The sun came out by afternoon after spits and spots of rain," and end by writing that there was no God.

I could see Anita trying to sound like one of these people, how the sunlight slanted through the cedars in the Blankenships' front yard. I could see her trying to be someone she was not. Not sounding false so much as empty, keeping herself out of the pages and letting someone else in, someone who had never heard of Mom's fossil collection or the way I could throw a football forty yards off a scissor kick.

"Is there anything?" my mother asked when I closed the book.

For a moment I could not speak, almost blaming Anita for whatever had happened.

17

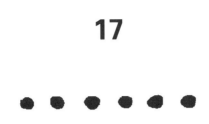

I put the diary in the top drawer of my dresser. I would be able to say I had taken good care of it.

Downstairs, I stirred some tuna into some tomato soup. The soup had some nonfat milk stirred into it first, and when it starts to simmer, the recipe calls for two cans of tuna. I don't like using the kind packed with spring water; it reminds me of what we sometimes feed Bronto.

There was a knock at the front door. Dad had a brief conversation in the doorway, and I heard the crackle of money, and that flat silence of cash being counted out. He hustled back into the kitchen with a large package wrapped in brown paper.

He began peeling open the wrapping before I could warn him. I had fragmentary mental warnings, too hideous to think: kidnappers sometimes sent body parts of their victims. But Dad was eager, confident, whisking away the last of the paper.

He stopped ripping paper and stared, putting his hands on his hips. "I didn't know it would be that color," he said.

"It looks fine," said Mother.

"I picked it out," he corrected himself, "but I didn't know it would look so awful."

"It looks good," I said.

"Do you really think so?" he asked hopefully.

When my dad gets into a mood like this, he has to be reassured. There were five flimsy boxes, electric blue sheets of my sister's graduation picture reproduced in black and white. At the top border was the word: Missing. At the bottom of the sheet was another black word: Reward.

Smaller lettering gave the Oakland Police Department telephone numbers, and our number, along with a description of Anita and a phrase that hit me: *last seen near MacArthur BART station at approx. 8:00 P.M.* It added further information, and I wondered which of Anita's acquaintances at the shelving company had volunteered so much.

The phrase bothered me. Even the abbreviation for *approximately* didn't look right. Anita deserved a more dignified poster, not something thrown together in such haste. Her picture looked more unreal than ever reproduced on this shade of blue. And besides—when she came home she would look at all this and tell us what a waste of paper it was, and how polluting the dye would be, deposited in landfill.

"The manager at Copymat suggested goldenrod," Dad said. "That's a kind of orange yellow," he added, making a face to show what he thought of orange yellow.

"What color is this supposed to be?" I heard myself ask.

"It's called Florida blue," he said. "I just stood there looking at reams of paper. Lime green, circus pink. And all I could think of was that satin dress she wore to the banquet when I got that award."

He had been Bay Area Businessperson of the Year, and the mayor had given him a wooden plaque with a brass plate. Dad had given a very funny speech, and we were all proud. It was the first time in my life I had ever worn a tux, rented, all except for the shoes, at Selix. We had all felt happy, and joined in giving Dad a standing ovation. Anita had worn a shiny blue dress, Florida blue, more or less.

"Two thousand five hundred of them," he said. "I'll swing by the office, grab some staplers. Not furniture staplers, the standard office kind. You probably want to hit each one with a stapler in each corner, so we're looking at ten thousand staples."

Mom and I did not say anything, but Dad responded as though we had. "That's not as many as it sounds. A box of Bostitch standard staples holds five thousand, a little box the size of a chalkboard eraser. Two boxes like that and we're all set."

The pot behind me sputtered. Little specks of

tomato and tuna appeared on the stovetop. I spooned the steaming stuff out onto slices of toast. The bread from the machine toasted well, but in odd shapes, not like the loaves from the store. The edges burned, and sometimes a corner that stuck out of the toaster stayed pale, not browning.

"It'll take half a minute to staple each poster," I said. "Not counting time spent finding a telephone pole to fasten each one onto—"

"And bulletin boards at libraries. And Safeways. We're going to plaster the Bay Area." He didn't like the way I had said *telephone pole*, making the words sound absurd.

I thought that hunting all over the East Bay for wooden poles would do very little to help Anita. Some neighborhoods didn't have telephone poles at all, only streetlights. Streetlight poles were made out of shiny metal or cast concrete. To affix posters to those we would need masking tape. "You put up posters like that for missing pets," I said. "If Bronto gets lost, we put up a blue poster."

"Bronto isn't the issue," said Mom.

"Reward." I didn't like that, either. It made her look like a fugitive.

Anita would have sprinkled some Kraft Parmesan cheese over each serving, and so I did, too. I could see why chefs at Denny's always add a sprig of parsley. The food looked bare and not very appetizing. It was dark out, early evening. I deliberately didn't look at the clock.

"The poster is great," I said. "That blue will get attention." Anyone could tell I was trying to be diplomatic, and having trouble.

Dad shifted the poster onto the floor with quick, sharp movements. His feelings were hurt.

"We can pass them out at BART stations," I said. "Put one up at every school in the Bay Area. And clinics."

"Sure," Dad said, very quietly.

I put out a fork and spoon for each of us, and a folded paper napkin. Dad heard out my report on the fire inspector without comment. I asked if I should go up on the roof the next morning to double-check the hopper and make sure it was empty of sawdust. He just stared down at his plate as though he did not recognize food.

Mother looked sideways at what I put before her. Her lab coat pockets were bulging with candy wrappers, and a brown and green Milky Way wrapper lay at her feet, crumpled. She was probably not hungry, but she found the spoon without looking at, and ate holding the bowl under her chin, sitting sideways like someone not completely committed to sitting where she was.

"We're not behind yet," Dad said. "We shipped out thirty-five today. We keep shipping, we'll be okay." Nightstands. He could still think about nightstands.

He got up slowly, and took his time getting over to the sink. He was wearing a V-neck undershirt and dress slacks with a nice crease. The shirt and pants did not look good together, the pants expensive and new, the shirt the sort of thing he wears around the house, torn under one armpit.

"I'm not really worried about another fire," I said. I felt a little guilty for even raising the possibility of a further anxiety in his life. "I'm just thinking."

"That's good," said my father. His glasses were off and his eyes blinked at me, not seeing me very well. There were permanent little indentations on the bridge of his nose where his glasses rested, twin little footprints, one on each side of his nose. He did something I rarely saw him do: He washed his glasses off at the sink, using soap and Palmolive dish soap and a big soft linen dish towel, a map of the Counties of Ireland.

"That's smart, Cray," my dad said, not really noticing what he was saying. "You keep thinking."

The phone rang again. It never stopped for more than five or ten minutes. My mother's parents had already called twice from Iowa; my dad's parents had both died when I was too little to remember. Each time the phone rang there was a surge of emotion in me, in all of us.

18

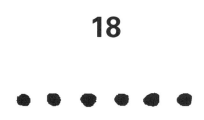

Dad answered the phone. There was always a hitch in his voice, a hesitation; this might be the call.

"It'll be on the ten o'clock news," he told someone. Not *she'll* be on. *It*. Anita had become a subject, a story.

He listened to the voice in his ear, nodding as though whoever it was could see the expression on his face. "I talked them into it. I had to push a little, explain that she was an honor student, still only seventeen." He was bragging about the influence he had with the television station. I didn't really blame him.

I didn't even ask who it was. These were Dad's telephone friends, people he talked to on the phone. Some days he could sit and talk for three hours to one person after another. He had called all of Anita's friends, taking his time with each one, checking off names on a list. Sometimes it seemed like he could have a better conversation with people he couldn't see.

When the phone rang later, as I was putting the dishes in the dishwasher, it was a surprise. Dad handed me the black portable phone he liked to carry in his pocket. "It's for you," he said, with just a trace of annoyance. He was nice about it, but you could tell that social calls to me were something he didn't consider very important right now.

"Cray, I have been here for hours." People like to say my name, starting sentences with it. I knew who it was and I felt myself go stupid. "I have waited one hundred years," said Paula.

"Christ, what time is it?"

"Almost ten," she said.

"I forgot." Dish soap all over my hands, dissolved foam running down the phone. I had not given her a thought all day. I didn't care very much, either. Maybe I wouldn't see Paula anymore after this. "There was a family emergency."

"I was experimenting. Deliberately not calling you. Seeing how late you'd be before you picked up the phone."

Still, Paula was a friend. "I'm sorry."

"This is how you really are, Cray. Wherever you are, that's all you think about. I almost admire it." She was ready to shift from impatience to anger. "You don't think anybody else is alive out here."

"It was an emergency," I said, giving the final word special emphasis. "It still is. I'm sorry."

I didn't want to talk about Anita. Saying her name seemed like it might be bad luck. The sound of her name might break whatever calm we were able to keep.

I think Paula didn't take my family especially seriously. She has one cousin who is a surgeon, and another in prison. She never came out and said it, but I think she thought my parents were hard to figure out, even a little amusing, wrapped up in their projects. But my tone stopped her.

"I can't talk right now," I said.

Paula sighed. It was a theatrical sigh, forgiving, dismissing. But I was a little impressed with Paula. She had enough sense to say good night and hang up.

My mother sat at the table, looking at one of Dad's lists, or maybe a letter he was going to send to the newspapers. She had a pencil in her hand. When she saw something on the list she didn't like, she circled it. It was their mailing list, a computer printout they used at Christmas, everyone they knew.

Dad brought one of the portable televisions from upstairs and set it on the sink next to the bread machine.

What was Mother doing, I wondered, proceeding in her silent, methodical way? I could guess. Following Dad's urgings, sending Anita's image to everyone

111

who lived within two thousand miles. Or even farther, to Dad's buyers in Eastern Europe, his designer friends in Japan.

Channel Two's Award Winning Ten O'clock News went on for an hour, ten to eleven, dragging in news from around the world to add to whatever was happening locally. I couldn't look at it. I went out into the back garden, that frontier of things my dad hadn't gotten around to yet.

Oakland, and the flecks of light descending toward the airport in South San Francisco, seemed to appear just as I looked, as though the world had been blank and dark one moment before I turned my head. In a few minutes it would be known, in every corner of the Bay Area and beyond.

When a player suits up for football he puts on a cup over his genitals, a mouthpiece between his teeth. Some players like the mouthpiece so much they carry it around with them, popping it in during math test, a transparent plastic smile that exactly fits the mouth. When it was all put together for the first time, helmet with its cage over the face, shoulder pads, thigh and hip pads, I felt wonderful. Even in the gray practice jersey with HOOVER HIGH stenciled on crooked, a ratty gray shirt that barely stretched down to cover my belly button, all I wanted to do was fall down.

I ran down to the thirty-yard line, down to the twenty, and threw myself on the ground, laughing, rolling, leaping up and doing it again. Even when the jayvee coach, Mr. Ernest, called, "Buchanan, get your behind over here," in his raspy little voice, I kept spilling, spinning, slamming off the goalposts, bamming into the other players. It was a wonderful feeling—nothing could hurt me.

Dad could have gotten sued for having all this equipment lying around, sledgehammer, post-hole digger covered with a tarp. What if a tax assessor or a PG&E man came back here, someone wandering in to read the gas meter, and he fell over the rusty wheelbarrow?

Was it over yet, I wondered? Was her face and her name all over the place by now? For the first time I felt myself lose control, out there in the dark, my sister's name, her face, broadcast all over Northern California.

I went to bed.

I listened to music for a while, finding stations that never broadcast any news. I used to fall asleep listening to music almost every night and wake hours later with my earphones still feeding me tunes.

I gave up and turned off the radio and lay there knowing that I would not fall asleep, that it was useless to try.

But I did sleep, a little. Sometimes when I woke I got out of bed and stood at the top of the stairs. I could not see my parents from there, but I could tell where they were. My mother's lab coat was folded and perched on the magazine stand. Dad had presented it to her as a gentle joke—my wife, the scientist. But she liked wearing it while she watered her plants, or sat in the kitchen writing letters.

She was asleep on the sofa, a box of Kleenex just beyond reach. The kitchen light was bright, and a dim shadow on the living room carpet was my father, head on his arms at the kitchen table. I don't think he slept much. The shadow kept moving as he straightened his back, slurped some coffee, put his head down again for a little rest.

He didn't drink coffee as much as he used to. He took Tagamet for his ulcer, and was supposed to eat five or six small meals a day. Listening to him sip coffee could be annoying. He sucked it in, a long inward whistle, followed by a slurp. He didn't drink orange juice or milk like that—only coffee.

I dreamed about her. She thumped her way up the stairs and demanded to know how her room got so messed up. She called my name. She was already losing her anger. She wanted me to say something. And I would, as soon as I could rouse myself from this deep sleep. It was not like a dream at all. Only when I woke did I feel the falseness of it.

The Anita of the dream was the Anita of several years before, when she had had such a bad sunburn. Her shoulders had peeled all the while we were at

Lake Tahoe, little pink freckles breaking out all over her nose.

When morning arrived, gray light filling the bedroom, I slipped out of bed and got the diary out of the top drawer.

I had not wanted to remember the last words Anita had said to me, the evening before she vanished. Both of us were sitting on the sofa, the television off, Anita watching me search for the remote on the coffee table, pawing through magazines. We both saw it at the same time, the remote with all its tiny buttons lying on the floor beside the coffee plant.

It was late, Mom and Dad both upstairs, and we looked at each other, Anita giving one of her smiles, sly, in on one of life's jokes. "Things move around when you aren't looking," she said. She had a voice that was ready to take on any emotion, her voice colored just then with amusement and even affection.

"On legs," I had said. And she had made her fingers walk along the sofa, a slow, good-humored spider.

Was that the last thing she had said to me? Hadn't I said something in return, and hadn't I walked over to the television and turned it on? One more word. She must have said something else. I could only remember Anita stretching, elaborately, taking more pleasure in it than any cat. And then she went upstairs.

I sat there in my bedroom with her diary. I turned

the pages slowly, giving each page a hard look, searching. In all these pages, she was pretending to be someone else. There were quotations in the diary, almost all poems I recognized from reading I had done for English, Emily Dickinson. Anita's handwriting became especially neat when she copied out these lines. Her own words looked hasty, pressed into the page.

Some of the lines she quoted made me stop and reread, not liking what I was thinking. Three pages away from the last entry, I read: "The soul selects her own society, / Then shuts the door."

Beneath the lines from the poem: "Tonight. Again."

19

I found my mother in her office. Bronto was sitting in a chair next to her, and for a moment it looked as though the cat was giving her advice. Mom had opened several Jiffy bags, and the padding from the bags scattered over her desktop, gray dust. A stack of new books rested on her desk, new geology textbooks and magazines as thick as books with lists of articles on the cover.

I'm a different person early in the morning. Smells are brighter, sounds are cleaner. I can't get a grip on things, though, fumbling, slow but hypersensitive. I hate to go running early in the day because it's twice as much work, dragging my body before it wants to go.

Mom had a cup of coffee, a crust of what had been a turkey sandwich. It was like a morning weeks before this one, before any of this had happened. She carefully whisked the bread crumbs into her trash can with the side of her hand.

I showed her Anita's diary, opened it before her on the desk. She did not look at it for more than a moment, gave it one stony glance and looked away. She asked what I had found. Bronto stretched his neck and chewed on a corner of the diary, experimentally. I gave the cat a gentle push and he landed on the floor, looking serene.

She was hoping she would not have to read it herself, but I didn't say anything. She turned and looked at the page open before her. She lifted her shoulders and let them fall.

Then she read the two words, leaning on her elbows, taking as long as she would have taken with a beefy paragraph.

I showed her other passages I had overlooked at first. The word "tonight," circled, at the top of one page. "I promised" at the bottom of another page. Her real life, her actual feelings, exploded on the page only in tight little bursts. It was easy not to see them at all on first reading.

"So?"

I hate that. A person can give a whole presentation, logical and eloquent, and a bored listener can wipe out the entire argument by saying, "So?"

Besides, I could see the dishonesty in my mother's posture. She was pretending she didn't get my point, but she did. "There was something going on in her life."

My mother closed her eyes. Maybe she was going

to cry again. Maybe she was going to shriek. I was nervous for a moment, not able to judge her mood. "You have to know Anita," I said, very gently.

"She was always thinking," said my mother at last.

I was a little relieved. She was in control of her feelings. That was easier for both of us. "She had a friend none of us knew about," I said.

"I wonder if I really understood her," she said. She gave a silent, sad laugh, shaking her head, quiet bitterness it hurt me to see.

I wanted to say: she had a lover. There was a romance in her life. The only phrases I could think of were words Anita would have chosen, bookish but magical.

"A friend," said my mother in a flat, emotionless tone.

"A man," I said. Saying it like that I had to imagine this man, this shadowy figure with a penis.

"A man she wouldn't tell us about," she said, not agreeing with me, just letting me know she was paying attention.

That sounded bad. Anita was so frank with her opinions. The man would have to be someone she knew none of us would like or approve of. Someone almost frightening, I thought, someone who would convince her to hide from her family.

"Do you think I should call Detective Waterman?"

"Detective Waterman is very busy," she said, in a tone of mild scorn.

Her tone surprised me. I had assumed that my mother would appreciate Detective Waterman's efforts, and admire her as a fellow professional, a woman in a tough line of work. "I thought Detective Waterman seemed pretty nice," I said, hating my feeble choice of words.

My mother was about to say something ironic, but she stopped herself. She put her hand over mine. "This happens all the time," she said.

I knew what she was saying, but maybe it was my turn to play stupid.

My mother softened her voice even further, as though we had been disagreeing and now were getting back to normal. "Anita is missing. She might come home right this minute." She couldn't keep from pausing, to see if the front door was opening, steps hurrying into the living room. "We have to do what we think is right."

One of the thick magazines was open to an article, "Earthquakes and the Geologic Record." The author was Frances Tilling Buchanan, my mother. I knew how pleased she would have been on an ordinary day, how we all might go out to dinner at Jack London Square to celebrate. Now she folded a Post-it and put it into place, closing the magazine so she could look at it later.

"That's great," I said, my voice a feeble copy of the congratulations I would usually have given her.

"The article explains that some of the Bay Area hills

are upside down," she said. Sometimes she does this. She'll be walking along a hillside and suddenly say, "What an explosion!" She's referring to something that happened ten million years ago, the debris, eroded lava at her feet.

"One big earthquake and a whole mountain flipped?" I heard myself ask. I was using the voice of a much younger person, trying to stir up her mood, trying to get her thinking.

"More or less," she said.

I called Detective Waterman and left a message after the beep, telling her I would be at the factory most of the day. I felt like my father, briefly. He never leaves a simple message. His messages say he'll be at the factory until noon, in L.A. until seven, and in Chicago tomorrow.

Then I took the bus down to the factory. It was Saturday, but a half crew was laboring, and the shipping department was crazy, two trucks waiting. The standard-sized boxes ran out, and so the shipping people had to make cartons out of great sheets of cardboard.

They cut the cardboard with a grip-razor, a handle with a dazzling-sharp edge sticking out of one end. One slash and half the cardboard fell away. A bend or two, and a nearly entire box stood there, waiting to be taped up. They sealed a carton around each nightstand, with padding at the edges, strips of a new kind of foam rubber, biodegradable. Although I wasn't as fast as some of the workers, a little nervous about cutting myself, after a while I picked up speed.

The buzzer sounded for lunch break and I headed for Dad's office. He was not there. Barbara was in the office, tapping the eraser end of a pencil on the computer screen. She had arranged the pink while-you-were-out slips into rows. She waved a pink message slip at me, and I took it.

Detective Waterman had returned my call. There were two numbers where I could reach her, and I tried both of them, trying not to disturb any of the papers on my dad's desk.

"Waterman," she said when she answered the second number.

Something about answering the phone like that sounds so impressive. No "Hello," no "Can I help you?" Just a last name. I explained who I was and why I had called.

"Diaries can be the key," said the detective.

As I described the words, the few phrases, she said, "Uh-huh" and, "Is that right," but she didn't say, "I have to get my hands on that diary."

"It's good to keep our minds open," she said at last. She was starting a car and releasing the parking brake as she talked; I could tell by the background noise.

"Ask if anyone saw her getting into a car," I suggested. "Walking along the street with a man." I almost added: holding hands. "She must have gone someplace with whoever it was." She must have loved him.

I knew it sounded lame, and I couldn't keep the frustration and disappointment out of my voice.

"If you come up with a name," said the detective. "A phone number. An address. You are not wasting my time, Cray. And you aren't wasting yours, either. Keep thinking."

20

Jesse was showing one of the new workers where he should keep his lunch next time, not on top of the glue press, where it had fallen behind the equipment and would be eaten by mice during the night. Jesse's body language was easy to read; there was still hope, his gesture said, indicating the outdoors where a lunch wagon had pulled up beside the shipping room.

Beside the factory is a yard of piled-up lumber, some of it just arrived and pale, leaking sap from the ends, little amber blisters, some of it weathered and gray, warped, two-by-fours tumbling off the stack because they won't stay straight. The first time my dad had shown me this open-air storage he had said only two words. He had nodded in the direction of a stack of cracked plywood and said, "Black widows."

The spiders were easy to find. I discovered one just then, over by a bucket of tar. The bucket was unopened, but I knew what was inside. Dad sent a crew up every year before the rainy season. They would pop open a bucket like this, hammer on the bottom until the black cylinder of glassy tar fell out, and they would melt tar down and use it to seal cracks in the roof. They never got them all. Every time it rained, drops found a way in, a whisper of water.

I knew there must be another ladder around somewhere, but there was only this one, the rungs overscribbled by the messy web of a spider. She hung in the shadow, a glittering ebony creature in mid-dark. Only when I stepped to one side did her forgetful-looking web catch the light again, a tangle, hairs left in a brush.

Anita would wonder why I had to do it harm. I would argue how dangerous it was, and I would be right. But I stood there making noise, kicking the ladder, clearing my throat, and actually talking out loud, telling the spider that I was sorry but I had to ruin her web.

The ladder was wood, each rung cobwebby, dangling a moth cocoon or a wisp of trash. I leaned it against the roof and began to climb. Each rung creaked. All the way up I told myself that the ladder was strong enough to hold my weight.

The factory roof is paved with tar paper. Wherever a skylight gleams, the roof is scabby with extra tar, all the way around the frame of the skylight. Ventilation pipes murmured, the voice of someone singing in Spanish erupting eerily from a pipe as I passed it.

The places where the fire ax had broken open the hopper were sealed over with bright yellow tin, the tin nailed into place. I clambered up to the edge of the hopper and opened a trapdoor. There was only a little sawdust, at the bottom, and the bitter smell of cottonwood told me that the light glaze of sawdust was fresh.

I turned to go back, and stopped. A big man, a silhouette against the sunlight gleaming off the foundry windows down the street, was making his way up the ladder. Only his head and shoulders were visible as the ladder shook and the man grew cautious.

"I think this is the ladder OSHA told us to destroy," said Jesse.

The Occupational Safety and Health Administration inspected the factory from time to time. Dad complied quickly with their recommendations, and I knew that, somewhere in the factory, there were at least two strong new aluminum ladders.

I didn't know what to say to Jesse. "Be careful. You weigh more than I do," I said.

"This thing is making all kinds of groans and moans," he said, not moving.

"I just had to see," I said, after debating inwardly how to explain myself.

"You just had to see if I was lying," said Jesse, easily, as though he was saying something pleasant.

"You weren't," I said.

"But you didn't believe me," said Jesse.

126

I told him I was sorry.

"That's all right," he said.

Some people want to make you apologize twice, just so they can enjoy it the second time.

"No, I mean it," he said. "It tells me something."

Roofs shouldn't be so ugly. Nobody ever sees them, so they are ignored when it comes time to paint window frames and plant flowers by the sidewalk. I found myself thinking just then that if I ever owned a factory I would put pink shingles on the roof, or nice gray gravel.

Jesse made me nervous. I liked him, but he knew things I didn't, and he was used to telling people what to do. He was taking advantage of me now, keeping me on the roof, squinting into the sunlight, while he stood on the ladder looking around, the freeway off toward the Bay, and the railroad tracks, our own railroad spur empty now. The two of us paused to take in the view, rust red boxcars in the distance, the plume of white steam from the tomato cannery.

"We're three days ahead of schedule," he said.

"That's good to know."

"You can go home now, if you want," he said. "Tell your dad I'm keeping my eye on the production chart."

There was some meaning behind his voice, something I could not figure out. "No, I think I'll stay," I said. "Maybe break up that ladder, make sure nobody ever uses it again."

Maybe I expected Jesse to be annoyed. He was telling me I could go home, and I wasn't going.

He smiled. Gold flashed somewhere in his mouth. "That's good, Cray," he said, like I had passed some kind of test.

Every time I stepped into his office, I knew he would be there, phone to his ear. But he wasn't. The trouble was that, as soon as I stopped working, I remembered her, and that hurt too much.

We weren't three days ahead of schedule. Whenever there was a shipment a square was shaded in on the big sheet of graph paper in Dad's office. There was a line in ink, where we had to be by the closing buzzer every day in order to stay on schedule. We were one day ahead, at best. Maybe two, I reasoned, if you counted today's shipment. That was the point of shipping nightstands on a Saturday—we picked up a day on the chart. And then tomorrow was Sunday, when the factory was always closed.

My dad never said the factory was closed, or open. He said the factory was "down." The factory was always down on Christmas Day. The factory was always up on a weekday. I left the office and went out to the lumber lot and broke up the ladder. I expected it to take half an hour, but sometimes I forget how strong I am. In five minutes the ladder was broken scrap. As old as the wood was, it was white inside, where the sun had never touched. I tied it into a neat bundle and tossed it into the Dumpster.

When I was done with the ladder, I went into the finishing room and grabbed a paint gun. We weren't just making nightstands. We were making chairs and children's furniture and dressers. Pink and yellow chairs hung from hooks. I worked the lever of the hose, like the lever of a garden hose, only what came out was a blast of blue, sky blue, Florida blue.

Someone handed me a mask, and I put it on, and after five or ten minutes, I was almost as fast as anybody there. I sprayed nineteen chairs myself, and by the time the buzzer sounded, fifty-three bentwood chairs hung overhead, turning slowly as though they were living creatures, all those brilliant colors.

When I got home that evening, there was a white van parked at the curb. Another van, I thought. No big deal, I tried to tell myself. I thought maybe it was another television station, but I stopped to read the lettering on the door, two big red letters: FC.

And beneath that: Find the Children: The National Center for the Missing

I told myself that this was simply more help. And we needed help—I knew that. But another part of me went cold.

21

● ● ● ● ● ●

"I can't believe it," said Paula.

It was only the third Dumpster, and I didn't feel like apologizing or explaining.

"It's sick, Cray," she said. "And it's sad."

"Just wait here."

She sighed, a show of patience. But when I felt back to get the flashlight off the floor she reached down and gave it to me. "Be careful," she said, opening my hand and slipping the flashlight into it.

The alley expanded. The farther I walked from the headlights, the emptier the place became, my footsteps echoing in whispers. I approached the Dumpster and froze. If it was there, I didn't want to see.

Look what you're putting me through, Anita, I told her in my mind.

Look what you're making me do.

I reassured myself that I was looking for her shoes, one of her books. And that maybe she would be alive, squirming, tied up.

Sour smells, decay. Bread, lettuce, old lunches. The sodden, pleasant smell was wet cardboard. Even the steel of the big Dumpster gave off an odor—cold, rust and iron. I told myself not to look. I found myself wanting to call her name. This was the employee entrance, the back way into the shelving factory. The place was silent, Saturday night, nothing happening.

The flashlight made everything look cheesy, ancient. The ribbons of plastic shippers used to confine bales of cardboard scuttled underfoot. This Dumpster was empty, too, only a few scabs of squashed cardboard sticking to the interior. The back of the factory was shut tight, steel doors that pulled down and locked. At one end of the alley, a Doberman was going insane at the sight of me, throwing himself against the chain-link fence.

Paula was waiting just as I had left her, calm, like a cat or a Buddha, in a place that would make most people nervous. I swung back into the Jeep, and she offered me a stick of gum. I took it and chewed for a while. One of her feet was hooked on the dash, the other knee over by the gearshift. Looking out at the alley behind the shelving factory where Anita had worked, Paula looked relaxed, as though she was looking out at a beautiful shoreline, waves, white sand.

I had pulled by her house, not even killing the engine, run up to her front door, and asked her if she wanted to go for a ride.

I left the alley, the clutch not slipping, the Jeep running well. I kept it in low gear, cars passing me on the left, headlights bright in the side mirror. This part of town looked better at night, the empty shops still and dark, the paint store looking cheerful, all the different shades of gray and brown we could paint our interiors.

A prostitute pivoted on the corner, tight skirt, red blouse. Sometimes they work MacArthur, near the motels, and then the police cars cruise once too often and they drift up a few blocks. They move around a lot, walking tight little circles, standing still, then swinging into action again. Men think with their eyes—that seems to be the theory.

The downstairs of our house was taken over with flyers in boxes, the national movement for finding lost people having just found itself a new member, my dad trying to read and digest every single statistic. Every now and then, he read a phrase aloud. "The exploitation of children increases every year," he would read, pacing as he turned pages. Mother had sat there watching him, not taking her eyes off him for a second.

"The anonymous urban wasteland," he read. "Christ." I couldn't tell whether he approved of what he was reading or was just caught up in a frenzy of information, the way he gets when a new glue is discovered that will seal the plastic on the dressers twice as fast and at half the cost.

"Stop and take a look," Paula said as we passed the woman in the red blouse.

I was taking it slow, up Telegraph Avenue. At first it was all storefronts, the kind of store that barely stays in business, kitchen tile shops, locksmiths, a big plywood cutout of a key, hand-lettered CLOSED.

"She won't charge you anything if you just park and say hi," said Paula.

I couldn't tell Paula that prostitutes embarrass me. Just seeing one makes me feel like looking in the other direction. Partly because the theory is right—I do think with my eyes, and sometimes I wish I didn't.

As we reached the Oakland-Berkeley border, there were groceries, restaurants. We passed the empty windows of T-rama, the shop where Anita had her dead-animal T-shirt made.

"This is where I saw the naked man," said Paula.

"In the crosswalk?" I asked.

"He was walking along with no pants on and no shirt on. But he had his shoes," said Paula.

I had heard the story before. "This guy was completely naked," I said, just to keep her talking. I appreciated her company, and Paula was happy as long as she was telling a story, or trying out some of her words. She was wearing a baggy sweater that must have once belonged to one of her brothers and a pair of cutoff jeans. I found myself realizing that her hair was much longer than it used to be, all the way to her shoulders.

"But not having fun. I could tell by looking at him," she said.

"He was disoriented," I said. The flavor was already gone from the chewing gum. I tossed the wad into the street.

"Can you imagine being so mental you would put on your shoes but nothing else? Just walk out of your house?"

"His feet hurt." I didn't want to hear about a man losing his mind.

"This was a man maybe your dad's age. Could have been your dad's brother." Paula and I went to the Oakland Zoo once, and Paula kept wandering back to the monkey house, hoping to see one or two of them taking advantage of their frisky nakedness.

"He walked out and noticed the splinters in the steps, or the sidewalk hurt." I had to make this story sound less pathetic than it was. "Maybe he kept a pair of slip-ons by the front door. It was natural for him to put his feet in his old tennis shoes and shuffle on down to the mailbox."

"You think Anita left work and went up Telegraph Avenue. Maybe took a bus into Berkeley. Or maybe she got a ride."

I was not happy at the way Paula put it. "We can't search every street in North Oakland," I said, admitting that, if she was getting impatient, I couldn't blame her.

"If she came up here and met a friend . . ." Paula said. She was giving me a break, letting me fill in the silence myself. "Maybe she doesn't want to be found."

"Maybe not."

"*Lussuria,*" she said. "Italian for lust. Cray—she's probably all right. You're just torturing yourself. Your whole family is going crazy. She's probably having the most wonderful time in her life."

"She wanted something to happen," I said, trying to agree with her. "She expected it. An exciting adventure."

"With a man."

Paula said she wanted a burrito supremo.

"Are you sure?" I asked.

"You'll want something like that, too," she said.

I looked up at the board, the menu written in yellow chalk, and I didn't want anything. The man behind the counter smiled with surprising warmth. He was just doing his job. I knew that feeling—how he would look at the clock from time to time, looking forward to closing the restaurant, mopping the empty, peaceful place. But he enjoyed certain moments, too, joking with his fellow workers, being friendly to the customers. I finally ordered a side of guacamole, just so Paula wouldn't have to eat the legendary Consuelo's Cafe killer burrito without company.

"My family would just be getting around to worrying," she said. "My dad would just be starting to think that it had been two or three days since he'd seen my face around the house. Your family is so intense."

"Tense," I corrected her.

"Both," she said.

I ate a corn chip. Paula had to wait for her order; it probably took three people half an hour to make a burrito that size. I pushed my guacamole to the middle of the table, sharing. I could never tell if Paula was intelligent or only flashy. Conversation had never been important between us, except when Paula did all the talking.

"She could walk though that door," she said. "Right now, starving for a plate of chicken flautas."

"She would have called," I said, the cutting, quiet tone I use when I am warning someone to stop chattering.

The man at the counter called Paula's number. Her burrito supremo was huge, about the size of a loaf of bread. She prodded it with the fork, letting steam out through the small holes she made. It was wrapped in a flour tortilla, pale, wrinkled. The table was a battlefield of other diners' drinks, their salsa, their chicken tacos.

"A big mistake," she said, putting down the tray.

"I know you can do it."

"I'm going to need your help," said Paula, looking down at her dish.

"It's the size of a small person," I said.

"It scares me to look at it," she said.

Music broke into the murmur of voices, brassy, trumpety Mexican music, syrupy stuff, the sort of music designed to make people order one more beer.

For a moment I forgot. I was happy.

22

● ● ● ● ● ●

Paula's house was full of light, every window ablaze. Shadows passed the living room curtains, a house full of brothers and uncles. Her family gathered to watch television, warning the good guy to watch his back, cheering, pizza crumbs flying from their mouths, when a bad guy got blasted to red soup.

I told her I didn't want to go in, and she looked at me a little sadly. There had not been much physical affection between us this night, although I had eaten the last of her burrito, just to help out. If I went out even once with Kentia, I know we would have to go somewhere with white tablecloths, fresh flowers, tiny portions of roasted quail.

"I wasn't sure whether to give you this," Paula said. She tugged at her back pocket and paper crackled.

It was an envelope, and all the way home it kept the curve of Paula's body as it rocked beside me on the empty seat.

———

When I eased the Jeep up the driveway, no visiting vehicles were parked in front of the house. The front door was ajar and I had the feeling something was happening, a meeting, or Dad off on an errand.

He doesn't go out for a jog or a walk, or take a drive. He runs errands. But I walked through the door, alert to any clue, and there was Mother, hands on her hips looking big, wearing her lab coat and a pair of jeans. There was a space of time when no one spoke or moved.

"You knew better, Cray," she said finally, her voice a rasp.

It took me only a split second, but for that brief time, I didn't understand. "It's ten minutes after ten o'clock," I said. "I said I would have the Jeep back at ten-fifteen."

My dad popped into the room. It was very much like him to appear so quickly. He looked at me for a moment as though he were going to draw a picture of me, a long look, his head tilted back.

"You knew better," she said, barely above a whisper.

She did not bother moving quickly. She took her time, made her way to the stairs and took each step in turn. This was how she had moved many months before, when the weight finally peaked and the doctor told her she would risk stroke or diabetes if she didn't begin to lose. My father stood there and I watched her, all the way to the top of the stairs. She had not put all the weight back on in two days, but her face was puffy and her skin was flushed and there was a heat in the room, her body heat, the kind of heat I could feel when she had been eating, her metabolism running double-time.

She passed into the shadows of the hall. Her door rattled. After a brief silence the door slammed. A muffled crash came from her office. She did this when she was upset—grabbed a chair and threw it. And then she sat down wherever the chair happened to be, planted herself and didn't move.

I stood there, touching my hair, scratching my arm, feeling like a guilty person pretending to be innocent. Then I turned and shut the front door, hard. There was a good silence for a moment, solid, a presence in the house. We could go on like this for a long time. When Anita and I had a fight, this was how it was, taking positions in the house and ignoring each other, aware of every sound.

"You have to be extra careful," said my dad.

He spoke deliberately, having trouble with the words: *Ya hafta be.* I have never seen my dad drunk, and I thought this was a first, something to put on a page of my own diary, if I kept one. But when I drew closer to him I saw how tired he was, too, tired all the way through, weak with it. And brilliant with it, too, a clutch of papers in his hands, photocopies of Anita's vital stats—date of birth, weight, blood type.

"You drive in back of the place she worked." He was

too burned out to make the words sound like a question. It sounded like a wooden command, a zombie giving an order.

"Oakland Scavenger already picked up," I said.

These words did not seem to make sense to him. The trash in Oakland is collected by a company proud of this ugly name. The word *scavenger* sounds terrible to me; I picture vultures fighting over scarlet bones.

He gave a little nod at last. "I don't know why I even suggested it," he said.

I must have smiled wearily, or made some sign. It had been a difficult thing to do. My dad said, "Thank you."

I did not respond at once, surprised. "I also drove up Telegraph."

"But she wouldn't be—" He couldn't say: She wouldn't be lying dead on the curb. I began to feel it was wrong for him to press that flashlight into my hands and suggest I look for Anita behind the shelving plant. What if I had found her? What a cruel thing to make a brother do, discover the corpse of his own sister.

"I bet that's how police find people sometimes," I said. I couldn't stay angry with him. I was even trying to make his attitude sound reasonable. "By looking."

"You go on up and talk to her," he said.

"Dad, you have to rest."

"Have you thought about what you're going to do?"

he said. He was wearing his V-neck undershirt, the V torn a little, a ragged Y, and a very nice pair of pants, one of his suit pants, navy blue with faint pinstripes.

I didn't have any idea what he was talking about.

"Now," he said.

"Tonight?"

"From now on," he said.

Because you're all we have, he meant to say. The college you go to, the job you take up, your future—it was all my parents had left. For the first time in a long while, I found myself thinking about football. Thinking about touchdowns and perfectly thrown passes gave me no pleasure.

I wanted to tell him she was going to come back. I heard myself say, instead, "They're going to find her."

In one of the museums in San Francisco, there was a room no one could go into. All a visitor could do was stand in the doorway and look.

I loved this room. I saw it on field trips in third grade and again in seventh, and on visits with my family, while everyone else marveled at the aquarium or the skeleton of the allosaurus.

It was an eighteenth-century room, with a desk and a quill pen, and delicate chairs, and wooden panels on the wall. The window's shutters were open, and there was a view of something, a blank wall, I think. It was supposed to remind us of the place that wasn't there anymore, an eighteenth-century town.

Anita's room was like this. We should put a rope across it, one of those chains wrapped in velvet. Only the museum curator would ever enter to repair, to restore, to keep it the way it had been. I had to reach into the dark to find the light switch, and then I could stand at the line where the carpet changed, from worn hall carpet to new gray, Anita's choice when we visited the Carpet Coliseum.

It would take some work. Mother had left the room looking cluttered, books tumbled off shelves, drawers half-pushed-in. Unless that was what we decided to preserve—the way her room looked after the first, quick search.

Of course, I reminded myself, Anita herself would be here soon, to put her hands to her head and shriek theatrically, "What a mess!" But she would not really mind. She would understand and forgive. Anita would have a story to tell.

I closed the door to Anita's room and walked up the hall, to my mother's office. I knocked at her door. There was no sound. I turned the knob, and to my surprise it was not locked.

My mother was sitting at her desk. She was looking at the blank computer screen. The crookneck lamp was on, light gleaming off paper clips and pencils. A drawing had fallen out of a file, a leaf, drawn to scale, three centimeters of a leaf like the kind people put into their spaghetti sauce, except this leaf was millions of years old.

143

Sometimes I just wanted time to stop. I told her I was sorry I caused her to worry, and she took hold of my shirt front, a handful of cloth, shaking her head, and I was a little frightened of what she might say.

She was sweating and breathing hard.

"I know I wasn't fair to you," she said. "None of this is fair to any of us."

"We have to look in her room again," I said.

She looked up at me. Maybe there was a little hope in her eyes. She didn't speak. We both wanted the hope to last. At last she asked, "Why?"

"Because that journal isn't really much of a diary," I said, feeling bright and fake.

She let go of my shirt, but I could see the imprint of her hand there, bunching the cloth. "It's an exercise book," my mother said, almost proudly. "Anita was developing her mind."

"Detective Waterman said she needed our help. I called her, and she was very nice." I didn't like this tone of voice, eager, plainly lying. "She said that cases like this usually turn on the discovery of a name or an address. We have to look for notes and letters. Maybe another diary." I wasn't exactly lying—I was exaggerating, wanting to give my mother something. "She said it was the best thing we could do to help."

"You look, if you want to," she said. She saw my hesitation, and added, "Go ahead."

"You're an expert at finding things," I said.

She said, "Yes, I am."

23

• • • • • •

I opened the envelope Paula had given me.

"I know you and your sister are so close," the note began. It was a pale blue sheet of paper, matching the envelope, borrowed, I imagined, from Paula's mother.

"Close," the note went on, "and so alike each other." This was the way she put it, a little awkwardly, but I could hear her voice as I read. "It must be like having your own body out there lost. It makes me think how much I underestimate you, when I heard you say it was an emergency. The tone in your voice made me think I was starting to know you, after all this time."

Paula makes a little triangle over the *i* instead of a dot.

I wanted to search Anita's room right then. What I really wanted was to tell Anita how ignorant Paula was, how frustrating. There was no way Paula had been underestimating me. I was the one who had understood Paula, figured her out and got tired of her.

Besides, I was nothing like my sister. I wasn't going

to go to bed. I was going to stay up reading and lis-tening to an old CD my dad had bought in a half-price store on Solano Avenue, sound effects, a honey bee buzzing, pistol shots, a jet taking off, a horse race. A long list on the back gave the running time for each effect—four seconds for the bee, five for the pistol, one minute and four seconds for the freight train.

I fell asleep in my clothes.

Anita had found a photo of a dead wildebeest in a na-ture magazine. The animal had been killed by poach-ers for its horns or its hooves. The creature was decaying, mostly skull, but with a few ribbons of skin left, its eye holes staring.

Anita had ordered a T-shirt with this photo printed on it, and it was one of the few times my mother had lost her temper with Anita. "You are not wearing that shirt to the ballet," Mother had said. It was almost Christmas, and we were all driving over to San Fran-cisco to see *The Nutcracker.*

Anita said we were celebrating peace while animals were being slaughtered. Mom said that was true but beside the point. Anita ended up wearing it, but under her suede leather jacket. Now and then she would give the zipper a tug and we could see more and more of the neck bones, the empty eyes. Sometimes I couldn't tell if Anita was absolutely serious, or if she just had a very dry sense of humor.

I realized this was an earlier Anita, an Anita of a couple of years ago. Actually, wearing the shirt had been a challenge. People in malls had trouble giving the right change, having to count out the coins carefully with a dead wildebeest sticking out at them.

That was another feature of the T-shirt. It was a little too small for her, shrinking even when she used Woolite and cold water in the bathroom sink. For the first time I realized how grown Anita was getting— how full-figured, I mean. She did not have unusually big breasts, but I knew how men would see her, whisking her hair out of her eyes, sexy inside her dead-animal shirt.

It was the next day, morning, and the house was quiet. The bedroom light was still on, pale and useless in the daylight.

I didn't have to look—I knew Mother was still in bed, not asleep, just staying there. If Dad is in the house, the place feels different, something shifting, moving around, restless in some corner.

The house was still. I entered Anita's room and I had to murmur a silent apology, like a prayer. The T-shirt was still there, hung in her closet so long the neck hole was oblong. Mother must have seen how the closet was full of clothes, nothing missing.

The dresser was easy, waltzing it out into the middle of the room. The carpet where it had been was scored with the outline. The drawers came out, and I unpacked each one gently, underthings and pearl-button denims, frilly see-throughs and Nike terry-cloth sweatbands folded together. My mother's search had left key rings and wooden birdcalls tangled together.

I laid the dresser flat and felt along the unvarnished wood and the single, empty husk of a moth cocoon. The bed was not so easy, the headboard askew as I gave it a nudge. Every bed is a kit, slotted together, even a bed that has stood glued together in one place for years will fall apart if you nudge it the right way. I was very careful, turning over the mattress, feeling the undersides of the rails, feeling under the bedposts, turning over the mattress.

When I was done, I put it all together, carefully putting back the books Mother had left lying on the floor, making the bed three times, starting over, working slowly, getting it right, so in the end all the sheets were smooth, each blanket even, the coverlet perfectly straight, and turned down, welcoming.

I don't know when it became routine, when I gave up thinking each creak was Anita bounding up the front step.

Maybe it was that morning, Sunday, after an hour in Anita's room. I came downstairs to see my dad's oatmeal bowl already rinsed and upside down in the drainer, a stiff wire rack that holds the dishes upside down so they dry without being dried off with a towel. The pot was there, too, dripping a little bit onto the sink top. Dad usually likes old-fashioned Quaker Oats, cooked slow, with brown sugar on top.

Maybe as I sat there waiting for the toaster to pop, I remembered the dreams I had spent the night with, Anita in every single dream, talking. Sitting in the kitchen, lounging in the living room, laughing. Just being herself. Usually my dreams are strange and impossible, flying high above the neighborhood, or visiting strange places and experiencing the impossible feeling I've come home. The dreams about Anita were like reality.

Dad had left one of his legal-yellow pads on the kitchen table, beside the turkey saltshaker, a bird with holes in his back where the seasoning shakes out. "I've gone out with some posters," read the note.

The pile of blue posters was crooked, and I straightened them up so they wouldn't fall over. The answering machine had eighteen messages in its memory, but I didn't play any of them.

I think that Sunday was the day we began to avoid each other, not out of annoyance, but because we reminded each other that Anita was not there.

I spent most of the day up in Montclair, on the other side of the freeway. I walked—Dad had taken the Jeep, and it would take a degree in auto engineering to get the other cars rolling. Montclair is a district of Oakland with stone walls covered by ivy. The streets have more trees than our neighborhood, bushy pines and redwoods. There were houses like the one I taped a poster in front of, on the bus stop bench, a cute brown house with yellow shutters, a Mercedes parked in front because the Porsche and the speedboat filled the garage.

I ran out of tape very early, stripping the roll down to a bare cylinder of cardboard. I bought a new roll of masking tape and continued, taping the posters to streetlights, a ragged strip on the top margin, and a matching one on the bottom. Sometimes I went into a Laundromat or a convenience store and showed them the poster.

The owners always gave permission, and if it was only a clerk, they said the owner wouldn't mind. One man asked if he could have a few for his church study group; they liked to lend a hand to deserving causes. The owner of a Laundromat said I should leave a stack over by the magazines. So many people were friendly in a kind, quiet way, impersonal, like people when they see someone being strapped into a stretcher, curious and pained and a little embarrassed.

The only way to carry a big roll of masking tape for most of the day is to put it on like a bracelet. It was awkward, and sometimes I saw one of the posters fluttering away in the wind, or passed one I had put up an hour before and found it torn, not by accident. People walk around, and if they see something a little unusual, they just idly reach out and give it a rip.

Only one person confronted me. It was in a latte house, where people sit to read the Sunday *Chronicle* and drink big coffee drinks with milk whipped into white foam. Anita had said the culture was a little hypocritical about drug addiction. She didn't sneer when she said this, she just raised the point, meaning we should be forgiving of people with drug problems. She said nearly everyone over the edge of sixteen was a caffeine addict, but I liked the smell of coffee more than the taste.

I didn't want to cover someone else's posters, used computers for sale, guitar lessons, so I taped Anita to the bottom frame of the bulletin board, putting just a kiss of tape on the bottom, so it adhered to the wall.

I heard the man yelling and I didn't bother to look. People yell sometimes. It usually has nothing to do with me.

"You will *not* leave that *stuck* to the wall," said a loud, piercing voice. It emphasized the words in a searing singsong.

I turned, in no hurry.

"Take it off the wall," said the man behind the bran muffins, a thick-necked man with black bushy eyebrows.

He had a point, in a way. Maybe the shop had just been painted. Masking tape could stick to the fresh ugly green and peel away a little scab. He had a good point. No doubt the system was that new messages were supposed to cover the old ones, until after a

151

while there was a layer, weeks of lost cats and French cooking lessons.

But I didn't like everyone turning to look at me over their movie reviews. It was only half a room full, plus a few people at the round white metal tables outside, but every person was rolling eyes in my direction. I strolled over to the bulletin board and taped another poster right next to the first one.

I knew when I did it I was being childish. But not like a little child. Like a big one, someone about my size. I wanted him to come over and rip down one of those posters. I wanted him to edge past me and take hold of one right where it said *Missing*. And give it a tug.

The poster didn't say how much the reward was. It might not even be a good idea, I thought, watching the man with the eyebrows whisk off his apron. People were going to call up with fake hints, fishing for a piece of the reward. Maybe they would hope to get lucky. They might call up and say they saw her getting into a lavender Cadillac, or maybe pink, and it would turn out later that was the car the cops found abandoned at the airport.

Mr. Eyebrows slowed down as he approached me, eyeing the posters. He slowed way down, and stopped. He had a towel in one fist. I couldn't believe what he was saying.

He repeated it.

"I'm sorry," he said.

He added, "I didn't have my glasses on."

24

● ● ● ● ● ●

Kentia opened the door. Before now there had always been a polite smile, cool, few words between us. Now she spoke. "Come on in, Cray," she said.

Merriman's sister held the door open for me, standing aside, and I felt hulking and clumsy, even though I had put on a clean shirt and a new pair of pants. It was the sort of long-sleeved shirt I usually unbutton, roll up the sleeves, until after an hour or two the tails are out and I look like someone who has been doing somersaults. But I was all tucked in, pausing in a living room glittering with antique silver and dark, polished wood.

"I am sorry to hear about your sister," said Kentia.

I thanked her. I knew enough about wood to recognize mahogany. Bookshelves, table, a framed mirror. And I knew enough about furniture to recognize the custom-made leather sofa and side chairs, glittering brass tack heads. Every time I came here, they had new furniture.

"How are your parents managing?" she asked.

It was Sunday afternoon, and I had barely spoken to either of my parents all day. I had come home, still wearing the masking tape on my wrist, and changed clothes for my visit with the Merrimans.

"My mother is doing better than my dad," I said. I thought about my mother for a moment. Was this true? And what power did Kentia have, to make me blurt out such frank comments about my family? I couldn't keep myself from feeling my wrist, making sure I still wasn't wearing the roll of tape.

Kentia had always been cool toward me, not unfriendly, other things on her mind, about to enter her sophomore year at Stanford. I could not imagine her in a sweatshirt and Levi's. "I wonder why that is," said Kentia, her eyes gentle.

Maybe she was just being polite. Maybe she was feeling sorry for me. Perhaps something about the way I looked today made her take a few extra moments before she told her brother I was here.

"My mother doesn't know what to do," I said. It was impossible to describe the look in my mother's eyes. "She's used to dealing with information, and she doesn't have any."

"And your dad?"

Dad worried me even more, not getting enough sleep, thinking he could make enough phone calls and tape up enough posters to will Anita home. But I couldn't bring myself to say this, not even to Kentia's dark, warm eyes. "I think they're both doing as well as they can," I said.

I could juggle five oranges at once. I could cut a cartwheel around the living room and never break a single plate on the shelves beside the silver candlesticks. But around Kentia's slender presence, I felt like a large, poorly trained horse.

"And how are *you* doing?" she asked.

That proved it. She was just being kind. She had no real interest in me. But I appreciated her effort. It was easy for her, in a way. She had a soft voice and steady eyes, calm. She was peaceful inside, used to talking to graduate students and professors. But I knew she did not have to take these few extra seconds, books open on the floor beside a laptop computer with its bright screen.

Sometimes a person asks, and you sense the importance. It was a chance to share a part of myself. Her father was an executive with Clorox, something in the legal department. While he and my father were friendly, the contrast was always there, my father's glasses always glazed with sawdust. It brought out my loyalty, suddenly. I felt I had said something unfair about my parents, although I could not guess what.

"I'm doing pretty well," I said, missing my chance.

She knew it. There was just a tiny shift in her eyes. I was no longer being honest. I was just talking, being social. Was I mistaken, or was she a little disappointed? "What can we do?" she asked.

Maybe she meant: What can any of us do, in a world like this. Maybe she was being philosophical. But I thought she was asking what she, Kentia Merriman, could do to help my family, to help find my sister.

"I always thought Anita was someone who could keep a secret," said Merriman.

"She was always honest about how she felt," I said, my voice suddenly thin, scratchy.

"Honest, no question," he said, hesitating, knowing how painful the subject was. "It's just that I thought she could have a life nobody knew about."

I couldn't talk for a moment.

Merriman sat with one leg stretched out an a leather stool. His arms were folded. Maybe I shouldn't have asked, but I had to know. Besides, I had to change the subject. I indicated his foot with my eyes and asked, "How did it happen?"

Merriman looked at my own feet, my own black loafers. We were sitting on the Merriman patio, at the edge of the patio, before us a perfect green lawn.

"I had this pistol," said Merriman.

"An automatic," I said. I knew all this, but I was trying to push the conversation ahead.

He used to be the kind of friend you just sat around with. Now he seemed to want to talk. I had noticed this on the telephone, and I noticed it even more now. I didn't know Merriman the way he was now.

"Those twenty-two-caliber bullets," said Merriman.

"They look so small. You could hold twenty of them in your fist, like this." He closed his hand around an imaginary handful.

"They didn't put your foot in a cast?"

Merriman shrugged: cast, splint, what was the difference? He had his foot in a sort of sandal, something you would never wear to the beach, canvas and plastic. Only the crutches leaning against the potted cactus proved how badly injured he was.

"You didn't know the gun was loaded?" I asked. I hated myself, but I couldn't let the subject go.

"You know, if there is any kind of a gunshot wound you have to talk to the police," said Merriman.

"They ask a lot of questions," I said. I stopped myself. The line was something out of a movie, a television show. I had the dim memory of a dozen bad scripts, one bad guy complaining to another that the cops were asking around.

Merriman and I both seemed to recognize this. We smiled at each other.

"Are you going to play football?" he asked.

The question surprised me. Merriman was not assuming anything. He knew how different everything was for my family, and for me, until Anita came home again.

"I don't think I could have talked both my parents into signing the form anyway," I said.

Maybe I expected an argument from Merriman, encouragement, or criticism. He had talked his dad into buying him a black Mazda sports car, a convertible, so he wouldn't have to drive the family Mercedes anymore.

"It's only a game," said Merriman. I knew he didn't completely believe this. People had always talked about the Rose Bowl when they mentioned Oliver Merriman. They talked about the AFC and the NFC.

"That's right," I said. "And people would just say that I wasn't as good at the slant pass as Oliver Merriman. I couldn't live up to that."

"You'd be as good as I ever was," said Merriman, and suddenly he sounded much older, a mature man, an uncle, giving me advice in a dreamy tone. Maybe being injured makes a person feel old for a few weeks, makes him wise until the pain wears off. "I could tell, Cray. I watched those jayvee games, how you had a touch on the football. Not too hard, not too soft. You were about to flower."

And he put it in the past tense.

"I'll tell you how I shot myself," he said.

25

• • • • • •

Detective Waterman was late. I leaned on my elbows in the coffee shop in downtown Oakland, feeling out of place. Men in dark business suits plodded in carrying folders and briefcases, and women with tired eyes eased into chairs, slipping off their shoes under the table where they thought no one could see.

Detective Waterman was suddenly across from me, snapping her own briefcase shut. She noticed my surprise at her sudden appearance and smiled with her eyes. "There's a back entrance," she said. "I always park on Franklin, zip up an alley. A shortcut."

I felt into the big manila envelope and brought out the pile of papers, the photocopies of Anita's journal. I had overscored some of the words with yellow marker. It took a few minutes. I let Detective Waterman find these phrases herself, and waited while she leafed through the loose pages, then stacked them against the tabletop to keep them straight.

"We've interviewed her fellow employees," she said at last. "They were all very generous with their time. They work people pretty hard at American Shelf and Filing. It's one of two American Shelf plants in the country," she said. "The other one's in Toledo, Ohio."

She gave me another smile, trusting her smile, knowing it had power, the white streaks in her hair catching the fluorescent light. "Her boss was very helpful. Showed us her workstation, let us sift through all the inventories she'd been doing. The security service, American Protection, has someone on-site twenty-four hours a day. We questioned their staff, looked through their logs for suspicious vehicles, loiterers. Almost every business has a problem in that neighborhood, having to ask someone in a sleeping bag to move aside when they open the office in the morning."

I nodded, just to show that I was listening. I was a little impatient. Anita did not run off with someone who slept on the sidewalk.

"We got a list of her friends from your father. He called all them already, of course. She was in the French club, played tennis. It's been a slow process, driving out to see each of them. I hate interviewing people by phone."

"It would save time."

"How would they know I'm a real cop?" she said. "I could be a crank, calling up to be a pain in the ass. I could be the perpetrator, calling up to intimidate. Besides, people can lie over the phone better than they can when I'm looking at them."

I liked this, a detective referring to herself as a *cop,* saying *pain in the ass.* She was being open, taking a little extra trouble.

"But I'm surprised there aren't more friends," she said. "Anita is such an active, bright young woman."

"We are both slow at getting to know people," I said. "We're friendly, but not that close to our fellow citizens." I phrased it this way to make it easier to say, like a joke. I didn't like this, feeling defensive about our choice of friends. "The French club didn't sit around speaking French. They corresponded with French students, took a group of people from Avignon down to Disneyland. Anita liked to go places."

"Anita was president," said Detective Waterman.

"It wasn't like being president of the student body," I said.

"You sound jealous," said Detective Waterman. "Like you didn't want to share Anita with anyone else."

I didn't like the detective as much as I had.

"Your family is very important to you," said Detective Waterman.

For some reason this brought tears to my eyes. "You can see that she was meeting somebody," I said when I could talk. "Read the journal."

"Her journal means more to you than it does to me," she said. "Because you knew her."

"She comes right out and says it, on paper."

"I think that she knew we would be reading it, so she left out everything revealing."

"You mean you don't want these," I said, taking the stack of pages away from her. I had made them at the Copymat on MacArthur, not wanting the assistant manager to do it, standing there, putting the journal facedown on the glass, breathing that dry, chemical heat copiers give off.

She made her voice sound gentle, aware that my feelings were hurt. "I'll take them along. You're right. They might prove useful."

I felt like breaking up the chairs around me, metal seats screwed onto metal legs. I would never manage to break one, although I could bend one up pretty well if I worked at it. "Look at these lines about the soul. Selecting its own society, and then shutting the door." My yellow marker had slightly smeared the words, the Day-Glo yellow looking slightly greenish in the coffee-shop light.

"What do those lines mean to you?" she asked, an English teacher with handcuffs.

"It's Emily Dickinson," I said, surprised at the bitterness in my voice.

"I recognized the lines," said the detective. Her eyes slipped slightly out of focus. She was thinking. The lightning flashes in her hair were slightly yellow, the way white hair gets in the sunlight.

"And look at this," I said, an edge to my voice,

"from a poem about a snake." I sat back, waiting while the detective read.

> *But never met this Fellow*
> *Attended, or alone,*
> *Without a tighter breathing*
> *And Zero at the Bone—*

"Yes, that's always been one of my favorites," said the detective thoughtfully.

"The police sit around reading poetry, listening to the dispatcher," I said. I sounded spiteful; I couldn't stop myself.

"I was an English major," the detective said. "Cal State Hayward. My husband left me. I started working as a desk cop in Berkeley, got so I could knock my martial arts instructor down with one hand tied behind my back, so to speak, and now here I am."

"That makes sense," I said.

I didn't mean that her life story met with my approval. I meant that I was starting to feel a little better.

"How do you do it?" I said after we had both been quiet for a while.

"Find missing people? It's the computer that does it, really. We rake in names, numbers—"

"Knock a man down with one hand tied."

"I use my radio, get backup." She laughed, a private joke, something she knew and I didn't.

The restaurant was very neat, mustard and ketchup

containers lined up with the napkin dispenser on every table.

"I see what you mean, though," said the detective. "She might have had a secret boyfriend. You know what my next question is, don't you?"

I didn't.

"Will you tell me what you know, or do I have to figure it out myself?"

I couldn't talk.

"Brothers know things. They know a lot of things, without even being aware of it."

"You mean—if I went to a hypnotist I could remember all the details."

"I mean that you were used to covering up for her. And maybe—I'm not saying you are—it's possible you're doing it even now."

A waitress had not come near us, ignoring us in our corner table. Detective Waterman had suggested this place. She had a court appearance, she had said, and she would be happy to see me. This was her usual spot, I realized. She sat here across from someone two or three times a week, talking kidnappers and sex slave masters into confessing.

I said, "The case is going pretty badly, isn't it?"

Detective Waterman gave me a professional look, no expression.

"If I'm your best hope," I said, full of feeling.

"Okay, I'm sorry," she said, looking around, briskly moving the briefcase a little farther away from her chair, sliding it along the floor, looking around for the waitress. Little lines had appeared in her face, in her cheeks, her forehead. When she held her face a certain way she looked fresh, pretty. When she made a thoughtful expression, she looked worn-out.

"If you want to knock someone down quickly," she said, "you hit him in the back of the knee."

"With your fist," I said, not asking, just trying to get the mental image.

"With your hand. Or a weapon."

"A nightstick."

"I use a sap," she said.

I didn't know what she was talking about.

"A leather strap, weighted at one end."

I nodded, mystified but beginning to understand.

"You carry a gun," I said.

"In here," she said, reaching one hand down to her briefcase. She was businesslike, her smile gone, realizing she didn't know me very well.

"An automatic, or a revolver?" I asked.

"A Beretta. An automatic. All the police are gradually switching to automatics. Military cops made the switch years ago. Automatics are much more reliable than they used to be."

"So you know a lot about gun safety," I said.

Her eyes shifted briefly to one side, and I could tell she was wondering about my mental state.

I told her about Merriman.

———

Two nights later I finally called Paula. I needed to talk to her, but before I could, there was a question I had to ask.

"What do you mean, you *underestimated* me?" I gave the word a peculiar twist, stretching it out. I sat on the edge of my bed, Bronto sitting on the windowsill, looking out at the night. He had been washing himself and had left his tongue sticking slightly through his whiskers, absentmindedly, like a person forgetting to tuck in his shirt.

"It's just, for so long," she said, not sure how to express herself, perhaps trying to be polite, "for so long I had the impression all you ever thought about was sex."

26

● ● ● ● ● ●

My mother's parents flew out from Iowa for Anita's birthday. Nobody described it that way, although the date was right there on the Sierra Club calendar, a bristlecone pine at sunset—or sunrise, it was hard to tell which. *Anita* was written in, her block-lettered name filling the whole square on the calendar. Mom did that early in January every year, wrote in all the dates no one would ever forget anyway. Anita had been gone two weeks.

My grandfather owned and operated an eight-hundred-acre farm near Roland, Iowa. He raised corn and soybeans, and he had men working for him. Gramps was a beefy man with a grin, but sometimes during this visit, I would catch him without his usual expression and he looked red-eyed and unsteady.

He helped my dad mix up a load of cement, and the three of us poured the base—gravel and sand and Portland cement. It was hot in the backyard, and if we worked hard enough we reached the point where we were tired and could think of nothing but churning the wet concrete and then shoveling it out. The stuff had a wet, granite smell, like an underground tunnel. The concrete splattered into drops on our pant legs and dried stiff, comets of cement.

When we were done, we washed the implements off with the garden hose carefully, so they wouldn't crust up. We rinsed the hoe and the shovels, spraying the gray residue out of the wheelbarrow. A thin gray puddle fled out from the tilted wheelbarrow, but as long as we kept spraying, the gray mud fanned out and soaked in, and didn't turn into a stone puddle.

After that, the next day, we mixed up the top layer of cement, just cement and sand, no gravel, smooth gray frosting over the gravelly underbase. Both Gramps and Dad were adept at troweling the surface into the corners of each section, smoothing it flat, and then silking it even flatter with the blade of the trowel.

Bronto discovered the sidewalk, and left his paw-prints dappling across one section, gentle imprints. Dad filled in the Bronto-marks with a little cement he mixed up in a plastic bowl, soothing it into place, not talking about it, disgusted with the cat, but having too much respect for animals in general to want to throw anything at Bronto, who appeared now and then to look out from the back porch.

When concrete dries, it goes hard, but not the usual white gray. It turns the color of a sky about to storm. Sometimes veins appear in it, ghost lightning. Then after a day or two or more, the fade sets in, the surface giving up the darkness, and going chalky, but new-looking, fresh sidewalks all the way out to the weeds at the end of the yard.

The Bronto-prints were visible, a lighter color than the rest of the concrete. Dad and Gramps rented Weedwackers, and when we weren't down at the factory loading nightstands into Di Salvo trucking line rigs, we were all out there laying waste to the drought-bleached weeds, thistles and oats and foxtails that speared into our socks and bit the skin.

Mom wasn't so lucky, shut in with my grandmother, who had something wrong with her outlook on life. No one ever talked about it, but Grandma was always walking into a room shaking out a cloth, someone else's clothing, a sweater, and giving people a pained sigh, telling everyone without saying anything what a burden life was. If there were no clothes to shake out, she would take ahold of a rug and straighten it, grunting dramatically.

My grandmother came out to see us every year or two. She was always entering a room saying, "I just can't believe it," or "God give me strength." I always felt her disapproval, and knew she didn't like me, or my father. Everything my mother said pained her.

My grandmother would rearrange the magazines on the coffee table, or sit and listen to my mother try to talk about neutral subjects, the new Life Science building on campus, freeway projects due in the near future, and Grandma would not say anything at all, soaking up Mom's talk until Mom began to sweat and go pale, still offering subjects to entertain her mother, none of them working.

There were family meetings, stories of my mom when she was a girl, such as the time during a thunderstorm the telephone bit her—gave off a tiny crackle of lightning. There were tales of my mother in the Midwest, tornado warnings and dogs in fights with raccoons.

One evening we handed around the version of Anita's graduation picture that would go out to millions of households, along with junk mail, delivered by the post office. Her photo, reproduced in blue, was next to the picture of another missing person, over the words "Have you seen us?"

At moments like this, my grandparents did not have anything to say, and shook their heads, looking spent and heavy as they waited for the subject to change and someone at last suggested a drive to the Hall of Science, or another cup of coffee.

Anita's birthday was on the fifth day of their seven-day visit, and all day we kept busy, pitchforking the bare stubble, planning a garden, Dad making diagrams, how much would be lawn, how much vegetable garden. For dinner my grandmother made meat loaf, and we spooned it out on our plates, crumbly and crusted with a sauce she was proud of, ketchup and dried onions.

My mother had stopped even trying to carry a conversation, but I got my grandfather to talk about farming equipment, how dangerous the corn-shucking machines used to be. "And still are," he said, "if you don't keep your fly shut."

"Is this what we talk about at family dinner?" said my grandmother.

We drove them to the Oakland Airport, up Hegenberger Drive, and my dad kept talking. He told us who owned each hotel, what union the restaurant employees belonged to, and who their bargaining rep was. When we saw some egrets in the marshes along the airport, Dad talked about how well the fine white bird was doing, living in Africa and Europe and even India.

We were quiet on the way back from the airport, all of us exhausted.

27

● ● ● ● ● ●

Sometimes Dad drove off to the factory, late, after-hours. He would stay there until two or three in the morning, then sit in the kitchen with expanding files of documents he didn't bother to look at.

Some mornings he would be out in the backyard with his hands on his hips. He showed me what he wanted to have me rake, where he wanted me to put the birdbath when it arrived. He dug a trench for sprinkler pipes. He sketched plans with a pencil, maps labeled DWARF LEMON, FLAGSTONE. He paged through catalogs of lawn furniture.

"The sod I want to get isn't just bermuda hybrid," he said. "It's going to be hybrid bermuda hybrid."

"Maybe we should be thinking drought resistance," I suggested. "Sage and poppies."

He liked that, looking at me over his glasses, his face gaunt and hungry. "Juniper," he said.

He flew off to Omaha, after a layover at Denver, to

meet with Find the Children, and stayed longer than he expected, helping them plan a funding drive.

Before I got my graduation photo taken, my mother drove me to George Good's on Bancroft Avenue. I had told her that I owned a dark jacket already, and all she had said was, "Go ahead and try putting it on." I did, and it wouldn't button over my chest and I came down the stairs like someone tied up with a rope, swinging my arms until the sleeves gave a suspicious little rip.

My mother said, "Case closed."

She had put on more weight and had trouble if she got up out of a chair quickly, putting her hand out to steady herself. But she was staying calm, sleeping a lot, not talking unless she could say something pleasant, or at least useful, unlike Dad, who carried the phone around with him, even to the bathroom.

My mother and I went into the men's store, where neckties are lying under glass and men in dark suits with the slow manner of literature professors ask if they can be of any help today. It isn't like most stores, no one to help, everyone chewing gum. The store was soundless, headless dummies in tweed suits.

"We can't spend that much on a jacket," I said.

I liked the jacket. It was like the blazer someone would wear in an ad for Scotch whiskey, and I looked at my-

self in the mirror in my bedroom. I buttoned it and unbuttoned it. I let it hang off my thumb, flung over my
shoulder, the casual Californian. I draped it over my
shoulders, cape-like, sleeves dangling, the French
aristocrat.

I don't like having my picture taken. I didn't realize
this until I sat there, and Mr. Quarry, the photographer, marched into the room carrying a stuffed toy
bunny. He caught the look I was giving him and
laughed, "It's not for you. I take pix of little kids, too,
when I'm not snapping the entire student body of
every single high school in the city of Oakland."

I sat on a hard wooden stool, the kind they have in
art classes and biology labs.

"We want that back straight," said Mr. Quarry, not
even looking at me. There was an umbrella in the corner of the ceiling, something to do with reflecting
light. I had been here a few times as a boy, and had
never really thought about Mr. Quarry, how he smiled
so much he had trouble enunciating his words, his
lips so tight, the smile stuck into place.

"Okay, on the count of three. One, two. Think: sex!"
And there was a flash.

"How did I look?" I asked.

"Okay, here goes another one. Pow! We're on a
roll."

"Was that one okay?"

"Serious now, very intellectual. No, don't smile.
Turn your shoulders. Beautiful."

"Is my hair sticking out funny? Is there food between my teeth?"

"You're star quality all the way. Keep your chin down. Terrific. You and your folks will get a set of proofs in the mail, in a stiff cardboard envelope marked 'photos.' These are proofs, and will not be the finished portrait." He spoke rapidly, mechanically, like someone running an auction.

Only at the end, as he stepped into the waiting room to see the six students who were slumped nervously in chairs, did he slip out of character. He walked me all the way to the front door, and said, leaning against the door frame, "I keep hoping about your sister, Cray." And he didn't even look like the same smart, brisk man, his eyes suddenly tired, looking out at the sunlight, blinking.

The look in his eyes reminded me of how I really felt, all the time, inside. It was August. Anita had been gone three and a half weeks.

Paula was leaning against a parking meter on Lakeshore Avenue. "That didn't take long."

I unbuttoned my jacket but left it on. "Do you like Mr. Quarry?"

"He's not my favorite human being," said Paula. She shrugged. "He was professional."

"He took all my pictures in as much time as it takes to sneeze," I said, unthinkingly borrowing one of my grandfather's favorite phrases. "Decades from now

I'll look at my expression and I'll see that I wasn't ready. My face was just hanging there. I didn't know what to do with my mouth. Or my eyes."

"You look wonderful." Paula rarely gave me a flat-out compliment, so I was quiet as we walked past storefronts, to the Jeep. "What are you supposed to do with your eyes—take them out?"

The top of my body was dark jacket, navy blue silk necktie. My bottom was Wrangler's jeans, cut off experimentally just below the knee the day after school was out for the summer. "The school district should find someone who isn't I-have-to-do-everything-in-three-seconds."

"He was the same way with me," said Paula. "Flash, flash, good-bye. We'll come out looking pretty good."

Paula and I were trying out a slightly different relationship. We tried to talk more, about various subjects. She was set to spend the rest of the summer at the Language Institute in Monterey, a crash course in German for students with special talent in language.

I had to bend to one side to hook the key ring out of my front pocket, and it took a few seconds. In that amount of time, I understood why Mr. Quarry had irritated me so much. It wasn't only because my face would be preserved for history looking vacant and characterless. It was because he had photographed my sister.

———

I didn't want Paula to go to Monterey. It was one hundred miles to the south, but in a different world, sun, dunes, and old adobe buildings, and an aquarium with sea otters. Some dark-eyed linguist would sweep Paula into his arms.

Paula was changing. She had learned enough to pass an aptitude test. She had always pretended to know a lot of languages, and now she did not have to pretend.

"Let's give Bronto a bath," I said, shifting into third as I accelerated onto the far right lane of 580, having a little trouble finding the gear.

"Why?"

"I'm allergic to him because he's full of cat dander and dust. I can't pet him very much. My eyes swell shut. If I wash him, I can be more loving to him."

"Poor thing." I didn't know whether she meant the cat or me.

We were leaning over the bathtub, Bronto with his feet splayed against the sand pink porcelain. My dad had ordered this tub custom designed from a friend in the fixtures business who was on the verge of Chapter 11 and needed purchase orders. It didn't match the yellow sink.

Bronto was making a long, low rattle, vibrating.

Some of the Palmolive dish soap from the kitchen was sprayed into the tub, a green squiggle. Bronto stopped vibrating and hunched, stiff, unmoving. The water was splattering, too cold, starting to dilute the green soap. I freed one hand to work the hot faucet.

Bronto made his move.

Paula and I grabbed him, holding him down. "This isn't working, Cray," she said. Bronto snaked up into the air, and I caught him. I wrestled him back down into the tub, and Bronto began a new kind of low wail. His fur was sticking up in bristling wet spikes all over his body.

"This is a bad idea, Cray," said Paula, a new tone of voice for her, forceful but keeping her temper. We were all making noise—Bronto, Paula saying she was going to leave if this kept up, my own voice telling everyone to calm down, blood running down my arms, getting into the greenish water as it began to foam.

And I knew what Anita would say. I could hear her, so vividly I turned off the water and stepped out into the hall, Bronto a wet-spiked blur down the stairs.

What you are doing has nothing to do with the cat, Anita would say.

I almost called her name, feeling her there in the house.

28

● ● ● ● ● ●

There were still faded scratches on my arms when I walked across the field toward Coach Jack a few days later, walking slowly because Merriman was with me, swinging himself along on his crutches. Each time his foot touched the dry field, a puff of dust rose up and hovered.

Merriman eyed the scratches. Merriman and I were learning to talk about things and not simply enjoy each other's company. I was starting to be able to read Merriman's eyes, when he was bored, when he was happy. Now I could see a joke on its way.

"No, Paula didn't do this to my arm," I said.

"You're going to tell me the cat did it," said Merriman.

Coach Jack swung his head around to look at us through his dark glasses. He gave us a non-nod, a little jerk of his head. He was wearing aviator glasses and had a Band-Aid on the bridge of his nose, where the glasses rested.

The quarterback was a former wide receiver, a guy named Ortiz. He was barking plays, no one out there but Jay Pauahi, the biggest player at Hoover High, a transfer the year before from Hawaii. Pauahi was the center, snapping the ball back through his legs to Ortiz, who would dance back, cock the ball, look over the empty field.

Ortiz looked graceful enough, but he must need the practice, grabbing the ball from center without fumbling. Otherwise, Coach Jack would not have the two of them out there, faces glistening with sweat behind the face guards. The team was in gray, scruffy practice jerseys, the coach letting everyone else take a break. Players lay all over the place, the August heat finally settling in, smog, the field so dry there were visible cracks in the ground.

I had spent all day packing hardware. In three days we would ship the last of the nightstands. We were ahead of schedule, barely. I had not even bothered to talk to Coach Jack since our meeting. The thought that I had been getting ready to deceive my parents, lie to them and forge their signatures, had made me put football out of my mind.

Coach Jack punched my arm, a little jab. It hurt. "Taking good care of Merriman?" he said. He didn't bother punching Merriman, or acting playful with him. Merriman was one of those people no one fools around with. Even Coach Jack looked at him with a certain lift of his chin, like someone looking at a famous statue.

Merriman didn't say a word to Coach Jack.

"Just wanted to see how the team was going," I said.

"No news?" he said. He let the question hang there. No news about joining the team, he might have meant. He let it stay like that for a moment, letting me know he didn't like the way I had ignored him for weeks. "About your sister?"

Some people were beginning to become self-conscious about mentioning it, even a little embarrassed, as though the disappearance was shameful. Even Kyle had begun not to call so much. Perhaps people felt that there was the possibility that there was news, and that the news was bad.

But Coach Jack didn't mind slamming the questions home, asking, getting answers. "No news," I said.

Someone had called the police to say that a young woman who looked like Anita had been asked to extinguish her cigarette in the Oakland Airport coffee shop. Someone called my dad to say someone who resembled Anita had been shopping for steel-belteds at Grand Auto in Santa Rosa. There were a few other reported sightings. None of these sounded like Anita.

Merriman looked out at the field, half closing his

eyes against the glare. When a proper silence had passed since the mention of my sister, he said, "Ortiz looks all right."

"Ortiz," said Coach Jack, exasperation in his voice.

He turned and called, "Ortiz, throw the ball over here."

The ball was a decent spiral, way wide. As I chased it down, the ball bounding, hard to handle, I knew what Coach was going to say.

He said, "Ortiz, let Buchanan take the snap."

"That's okay," I said. Meaning: no thanks.

Coach Jack just kicked a little grass dust mouse, turning to look at the field.

I strolled out there in my Wrangler cutoffs and running shoes, and my new red T-shirt, STANFORD in stiff yellow letters across my chest. I loved the way the turf felt under my soles. Some of the field had come up in scabs, punched with holes from the heavy footsteps. Pauahi slapped my hand and gave me a grin, hand on one hip, breathing hard.

There were only the two other players on the field, aside from myself, but it was easy to imagine a crowd of grass-stained jerseys. I grabbed Ortiz by the sleeve and said, "Line up wide right."

Ortiz gave me a doubtful look from inside his helmet. "I'm just fooling around," I said.

Ortiz gave me a little hands-out gesture, pretending he didn't mind.

I lined up behind center and my hand went up to my

face. I had to laugh. I lifted my hand to straighten my helmet, give the crossbar over my face a tug. But I wasn't wearing a helmet and had not put one on since I was knocked unconscious so long ago.

I looked over the teams that weren't there, seeing it in my mind, the butts of my own team, the other team jacked into position, panting. Football players are always breathing hard, big athletes, tired after a few minutes of hauling themselves up out of the dead grass.

"P-twenty-nine," I sang out. That was a play number I was pretty sure didn't mean anything this season. I had left the jayvee team in the middle of last season and joined the varsity Wildcats in their blue-and-white uniforms. I had memorized all Coach Jack's plays in just a few days. The number meant that the receivers were to run down about thirty yards, and then slant in across the field, and try not to trip over each other if they met. There had never been a P-twenty-eight or -thirty. It was just a code, and sounded good, all of Coach Jack's passing plays ready to be turned into running plays if the quarterback saw his entire team coughing blood.

Pauahi snapped the ball before I expected it, dug it into my hands and then started his blocking routine, a dance with his arms up, his feet toeing the dry grass, a rapid turn one way and then another. No teams on the field, but Pauahi electrified, showing me and Merriman what an offensive center could do, all the players on the sidelines on their feet, hollering, caught by the mood.

This was where I usually stayed, right behind the center, while hands reached in and tried to face-mask me, bodies grinding together, gristle and joint, guys hurt and recovering and hurt again as they tried to keep from throwing up, hanging on. It was against the rules, but on some plays half of the players, defense and offense, stayed on their feet by clinging to each other's jerseys, shoulder pads popping out.

Ortiz was down thirty yards and made his cut, running across my field of vision, one hand up. And I had kept the ball too long, enjoying the feel of the little leather goose bumps and the Frankenstein stitches as I got a grip, stepped back, and cocked my arm.

I jumped. No reason. I needed something extra on the ball, and I was eager for some elevation. I was in the air, a scissor kick, and threw a terrible pass, my arm out of shape, the lame pass wobbling.

And not so lame. The ball wobbled just as Ortiz half slipped on a dandelion, the only plant still green on the entire field, the yellow flower springing right back, escaping the worst of his cleats.

When Ortiz got his stride back, the ball was bouncing off his chest, and he had to bring it down into his hands to keep it out of his face. So he spun, put a great move on whatever ghost was tackling him and ran. I had forgotten how it looks, a receiver clear, breaking as fast as he can.

I had forgotten what it looks like to see someone run, all out, nothing moving but one figure, all the way into the end zone, even if the field is full of jerseys, only one person there who is really alive.

Coach Jack gave me an expectant stare, taking off his sunglasses. "The team looks good," I said. Meaning: I wished him luck. That little sample of the game was sweet, but it did not change my mind. There was no way I was going to play again.

"It's timing," said Merriman, swinging along, kicking up dust out toward the Jeep. "No, it's not timing," he said, correcting himself. "It's touch. You have it, and it's driving Coach Jack crazy."

"Just a lucky pass," I said.

Ever since Merriman told me how he shot himself in the foot I was worried about Merriman, but awed by him all the more. He had explained the shooting to me sitting on his patio, just between the two of us, and I was still recovering from what he had said.

There was no defective safety, no forgotten bullet in the chamber. Merriman had sat in his bedroom with a gun he had rediscovered in his bottom drawer, a gift from an uncle. He had not known whether it was loaded or not, and in a spirited, mindless moment, he didn't care. He had stretched out on his bed, taken slow aim at his right foot, and squeezed the trigger.

No accident. I hadn't even told Detective Waterman the entire story.

We got into the Jeep, stainless steel crutches angling across the back.

"Maybe it was because you didn't want football anymore," I said. "Some part of your mind didn't want it."

"It's okay if you don't play football, Cray," said Merriman. "Personally, I would give anything to play quarterback this year." He looked back at me. "But don't let Coach Jack play yo-yo with your brain."

"He won't," I said, wanting to sound self-assured.

"He doesn't care about you or about your sister."

I was surprised at the tone in Merriman's voice, not contemptuous toward the coach so much as stripped of illusion. "He's a proud, sensitive man," said Merriman. "He's suffered and come back against all odds. He's learned so much about life he doesn't know we exist."

I wondered what Anita would think about the new Merriman, the books he was checking out of the library, heavy volumes about engineering, the great bridges of the world, the Roman arch, tunnels under seas.

29

• • • • • •

I jumped up into a Dumpster to pack down the cardboard scraps, a whole mountain of refuse Anita would tell us we ought to recycle, strips of plastic and torn-up boxes. Cartons gave way, collapsing in the depths of the steel bin. I tried to force it all down with my weight, gripping the sides and trying to make room for more, when a truck arrived, rumbling, backing routinely up the side street.

The big moment—the last of the nightstands was ready to be loaded, piles of neat cardboard cartons: THIS END UP. But from the start, things did not go smoothly.

The truck driver sawed his rig halfway back to the shipping department door, and then he started to have doubts. He stopped the truck, stalled it, and drove back, nearly all the way back to San Leandro Street, before the brakes gasped again and he shifted back into reverse.

Workers stopped wiping down the surfaces, cleaning up, the buzzer sounding as the truck was starting to look like an even worse idea. The truck scraped off the door handle of a Nissan sedan. The bright little door handle tinkled to the ground. The truck hesitated, got a new surge of power, and backed solidly into Jesse's metallic blue Chevy Blazer.

The truck driver got out, squinting, as though it was so hot and the air so dirty, it was no wonder. He was probably right out of truck-driving school, with a little scuzzy mustache and a bright blue-and-pink tattoo on his arm. For a while there was nothing but Spanish and Cantonese from inside the factory, the truck driver observing the damage, with no expression, climbing back into the cab, killing the engine.

Barbara must have been watching from a side window up in the office. Her voice boomed all over the factory, the volume turned too far up, calling for Jesse to report to the shipping department entryway, please.

But Jesse was already on his way through the shipping room, kicking the empty plastic bags that had fallen out of a carton, all new, ready for hardware. Jesse walked with his hands on his hips, a posture he might have picked up from my father. It's hard to walk like that and not look unnatural, and that's how Jesse looked, stiff with anger.

The truck driver was out of the cab of the truck again. He was not only examining the two vehicles, he was studying the end of his rig, which was scraped a little shiny where the door handle and the Blazer had each taken a bite. The driver had a blue adjustable billed cap and a white-and-red T-shirt with a Nation's Famous Hamburgers logo.

Jesse asked for his insurance papers, holding out his hand, not looking at the driver.

"I need to see the owner," said the truck driver.

Jesse made a gesture, bending his arm and straightening it, his fingers wiggling.

"I want to see the man in charge," said the truck driver.

"Mr. Buchanan isn't here," said Jesse.

Now that the truck driver had Jesse talking, he turned his back. He dug under the front seat of the cab, at eye level, and brought out a little black plastic notebook. He found the papers he wanted and gave Jesse one.

It took Jesse a few seconds. Jesse's work shoes were gloppy with old squirts of glue, crusts of paint. "I think you must have given me the wrong paperwork," he said.

"That policy is still in force," said the truck driver.

"This documentation has elapsed," said Jesse.

"What has *elapsed,*" said the truck driver, "is the parking rules."

The truck driver walked all the way over to the sidewalk, and there was an ancient red no-parking zone right where the sedan was. He didn't point, but he let one arm hang heavy for a moment, a minimal way of letting anyone watching know exactly what he was talking about.

"There's a story behind that parking zone," said Jesse, trying to shift into a more amiable style of conversation.

"A *story*," said the truck driver, so mad now that he had proven he was right, he was striding with a little jerk to each step, swinging up into the driver's seat, the engine grinding, starting up.

Mr. Ziff had painted that red no-parking zone himself, decades ago. It was a not a legal red curb, just Mr. Ziff with some paint that wasn't the right kind, weathered by now to red freckles.

I had the truck's license plates memorized, California and Wyoming and Arizona plates fastened to the trailer frame, so I could call the police if I had to. But Jesse jumped up beside the driver, onto the step beside the cab. He was hanging on to the door handle, searching for a better grip as the truck driver accelerated up toward the main street.

Maybe the driver would have slowed and stopped, having given the situation some thought. But Jesse was right there, his face on the other side of the window, saying in a loud voice, "Hey." Unexcited, like he was trying to get someone's attention in a situation without any urgency, all the while trying to hang on.

I could tell by the way the truck driver lost one gear and found another, how determined he was getting.

Having Jesse's face on the other side of the window just made him all the crazier.

Everyone on the sidewalk was shouting *hey!* People who didn't speak English were shouting *hey,* someone on the other side of the cab slapping on the door, running along beside the truck.

I jumped down from the mound of scraps and ran hard, getting to Jesse as he began pounding on the side window. He gave me a look and made his eyes wide, trying to be humorous about it, how he was going to ride all the way to Castro Valley standing on a six-inch ledge.

He would have to jump. He made a tense grin of effort, bracing himself to leap off the rolling truck and I told him to wait. I didn't shout. I just said the single word: "Wait."

I leaped in front of the truck as it ran the stop sign, the driver hitting the steering wheel with the heel of his hand angrily, giving me a blast from his horn. The truck brakes hissed, the huge vehicle shrugging sideways.

That was all I wanted—just a full stop so Jesse could jump off.

I stood to one side, then, while the truck driver jerked the rear wheel of his rig up the curb, scraping the mailbox, and shifted gears all the way down the street, past the shops that made kitchen cabinets and the foundry that made manhole covers.

"Some of these drivers get really tired, on the road all day and all night," I said, as though I knew anything about it.

"Don't do that, Cray," said Jesse, panting.

I must have given him a question with my eyes.

"Don't get run over," he said.

An hour later another truck slid into place, and a white-haired man with a stoop loaded nearly all the nightstands himself. He whistled a little tune as he signed the bill of lading, pressing hard so his signature went through all the copies.

That night we got the phone call.

Detective Waterman was at the coroner's office. A body had just been found off Skyline Boulevard, a young white woman, dead four or five weeks.

30

● ● ● ● ● ●

The call came just before dinner, tuna and mushroom soup over flat noodles. I made it myself, and stirred in some frozen peas toward the end. Mom came down from her office and shook some dried parsley flakes over it, and then rummaged in the cupboard and found a little red-and-white metal box of paprika.

It was good to see my mother taking an interest in helping, because usually she sat sideways and ate without talking, and then later, when my dad was on the computer in his study, sending messages to his Find the Children friends, she would be in the kitchen again, eating chocolate pudding out of the container, or asparagus soup, right out of the can.

She sat at the table, sideways, looking off at the collection of kitchen knives on the wall, boning knives, paring, carving, butcher, all of them lined up in no order, right next to the tool with a handle like a knife, but not a knife at all, a rod like a file, for sharpening the carbon-steel edges.

I spooned the mixture onto plates, and we were just sitting down, when Dad's phone made its electronic burble. It was a new system, a fax machine–answering machine combo, with a huge memory so Dad could listen to fifty messages at once. He had bought it at Whole Earth that week, and installed it in the kitchen, right under the calendar.

He picked it up, holding his paper napkin in one hand, and listened, and my insides tightened. Even before he was off the phone, my mother and I could tell this was not just another phone call.

He said, "Yes, Detective Waterman," in a stiff-sounding way, letting us know who he had on the phone. He listened, and his face went slack, nerveless, and not pale so much as shiny, a sickly light just under his skin.

He cupped the receiver in one hand, the napkin drifting to his feet. He told us the news after getting ready, working out the words in his head. "They won't be able to make positive identification because they don't have dental records."

No explanation, just that opening sentence, but we had already guessed what had happened.

My mother didn't say anything.

"The detective is giving us an interim report," said my father, cupping the phone. It was only then that he told us about Skyline Boulevard, and the phrase *dead at least a month* came out of his mouth like something he hadn't really said, words in a balloon, like in the comics, his lips half-parted but not moving.

My mother got up and dragged the chair over to the telephone, a gray Panasonic with a memory that could hold fax messages, voice messages, and half a ream of paper. She took the phone from my father, but my father didn't back away.

Detective Waterman was saying something, and my mother didn't shake or nod her head the way my dad did when he was on the phone. She absorbed the words and replied, "I have them here," as she leaned against the back of the chair.

My father blinked.

I carried the plates full of food over to the sink, clearing the table, slipping the unused paper napkins into the trash can under the sink.

"They are current dental records," my mother said, being patient, spacing out her words, the way she sounded when she explained to someone that the fossil record goes back hundreds of millions of years, not just back to Noah's Flood.

When my mother hung up, she felt around for the chair, and sat. Without looking in my direction, she said, "In my office, in the right-hand drawer, in the red plastic folder."

I was upstairs at once, past Anita's room, and in the doorway of my mother's office. By then I really understood what I was looking for, and I sat in my mother's desk chair, looking at the dust cover she always draped over the computer when she wasn't using the office, trying to calm myself down, trying not to make a mistake.

That was how I thought of it, the way my mother did. She knew that if we are careful, if we collect and store and file we will keep mistakes from being made, keep harm from happening. I knew why she had asked Dr. Ames, our dentist, to send these.

I found the red folder in the big drawer, the one that rolled out heavy, full of papers. I did not open the folder until I was downstairs, and then I thought— what if the folder is empty?

My father took off his slippers and put on dress shoes, rolling down his shirt sleeves, although they were still wrinkled where he had rolled them up. My mother put on a big wool jacket, and slung her leather bag with the strap over her shoulder, both of them getting ready, no one saying anything.

I made sure the stove was off, the black heating coils all cool. Once I had left a pot holder on a burner that was not all the way off and the quilted pad got a little tan along one edge. I locked the front door behind us. I thought I should bring something to read. I imagined myself in a waiting room, like waiting for an operation to be over, needing a story to make the time pass.

I rode in the back of the Jeep, looking backward, an experience I had always found enjoyable. The seat was bolted to the floor and had a seat buckle with a shoulder strap, and the arms of the seat had hard foam-rubber grips. You could hang on as the Jeep drove up and down canyons, that was the theory. But I found myself hanging on with one hand, even though the ride was smooth, my dad taking it easy on the clutch, all the way downhill, to the freeway.

In the other hand, I held the red folder. I did not have to open it again to visualize what was inside. The folder held black-and-white film paper clipped to sheets of paper, photos of molars and their roots, the silhouettes gray, like mountains captured by moon-light.

Anita told me she liked the peppermint flavor of the Novocain, the squeak of Dr. Ames's rubber gloves, being brave after the fact. She had had only one fill-ing in her entire life and it was there in a follow-up X ray, a jagged empty star at the crown of one tooth.

31

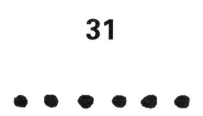

The Alameda County Coroner's Bureau is on Fourth Street, just behind the blue Health Services building. The coroner's bureau has no windows—a beige, faceless fortress. An old-fashioned blue sign, CORONER, sticks out over the sidewalk, with neon tubing over the letters so they show up at night.

Only in the rear of the building could we see an entrance, and that was where the white van with the sheriff's star on the side door was backed up, all the way into the shadows. We got out of the Jeep and I felt myself feeling just one pace behind my own body, my bones and my muscles a loose fit, clothes that didn't belong to me.

My mother took a long time accepting the red folder from my hands, putting it into her briefcase. Dad looked at the red folder and bunched his lips, an expression like a kiss, but thoughtful. Then he was off, hurrying to a side door, one with big dark letters, THIS IS NOT AN ENTRANCE.

He read the words after trying the door, and we followed him around to the front of the building. He held open a metal-framed glass door for us, a door much too small for a building this size. It was one of those doors that close partway and then close a little more, and then close almost all the way, and stay like that for a while.

There were no doors leading from the small lobby. A potted tree leaned toward the daylight, a broad-leafed plant in a brick red tub. The steps were brick red, too, worn brown in the middle of the stairs, and the banister was teak, I thought, or some other tropical wood worn dark.

We passed a door stenciled NO ADMITTANCE, and Dad knocked. His knocks did not seem to make any sound, absorbed by the metal door. He jiggled the knob, then went up another flight. My mother was breathing hard, dragging herself up the stairs, Dad hurrying on ahead, stumbling on one of the steps. He began to call out "Hello?" like someone wandering into a house before any of the other guests.

He knocked on another door, and a young woman with dark hair leaned out to look at him without seeming to understand, and then looked at my mother and then at myself, puzzled. Or perhaps she was not—perhaps she was tired, or nervous about something happening in her own life. I tried to read the look in her face as she heard my father explain who he was, mentioning Detective Waterman's name.

199

Someone came up the stairs behind us and said, "Do you folks need any help?"

We all turned, and something about us made him stop.

"These are going to be the Buchanans," he said over our heads, as though we weren't yet, but would be when he was done with us. He was a burly man with a red mustache and a star on his chest, right above a gold ballpoint pen, its clip over the front of his pocket. He was either full-muscled or starting to get fat. He filled out his shirt so it was tight all over his upper body.

The young woman's face softened into understanding. She said, in an accent I did not recognize, that we should go on upstairs and Detective Waterman would be with us soon.

"You just want to head up there," said the man with the star, assuming we could not possibly understand the young woman. "Take that next door, go on in, and some good people will be there to help you." He had a name on his chest, white lettering in a black rectangle, but I could not get my eyes to work, or my brain to register.

"We need to know what's happening," I heard myself say.

"I don't have any answers," he said, nearly filling out the entire stairway, side to side, "and I'm afraid there won't be any answers for just a little while longer, and believe me, I know what a strain this is on all of you."

How many times had this man stood in this building and given that sort of cop speech? I saw how little he knew about us, how many times he had trudged up and down these stairs, the rubberized radio antenna wiggling at his hip.

None of us were moving, arranged on the stairs, looking down at a big red-headed sheriff who had to tilt his head to look past me at my father and say, "My understanding is, Detective Waterman is expecting you."

I heard my father thank the man, and a door opened. Light from a room lanced down the stairwell, and we found ourselves in a room with chairs that had straight metal legs. It was the kind of room that usually has old magazines, but there weren't any. A satellite view of San Francisco Bay was framed on the wall, the salt flats at the end of the South Bay bright reds and yellows. Behind a steel-mesh window a woman with a star was making a gesture, indicating that we should sit down, as she picked up a phone and spoke into it.

The interior door opened and a figure entered the room, a tall, dark-skinned man in a suit. There was a pin in his lapel, a golden Oakland tree, encircled by the words TWENTY YEARS OF SERVICE. "Mr. and Mrs.

Buchanan," he said. He turned his face toward me briefly. "And the brother. I am Steven Wallace, the Coroner for the County of Alameda."

I went dry inside, solid, all the way through. We weren't going to see Detective Waterman, and despite my complicated feelings for the detective, I wanted to see her, a familiar face in this building of blank walls. I could see the wrinkles in my dad's face, the gray sheen of my mother's.

We shook hands with Mr. Wallace, taking a long time about it, my mother first, then my dad, then me. Even then, moving in little jerks, hardly able to stand upright, we went through the motions of behaving as though we knew what to do.

There was something dainty about the way the cororner perched on the edge of his chair, "What we have here is a young woman discovered five meters from a county road." A dash of white at his temples, a single white hair in one eyebrow. This man had just been inside looking at a dead body.

My mother handed him the red folder. He cleared his throat, opened the folder, and continued speaking. "It was among trees up near Redwood Park, and I must tell you we need to be very careful."

I couldn't help the way my mind worked. I couldn't help wondering why they had to be careful, like the body might blow up. I took my mother's arm. It was wooden, heavy, my mother staring at the coroner's knee.

"In these particular circumstances, fingerprints are not an option," said the coroner. He studied the X rays as he spoke. Then he reached into his breast pocket and shook out a pair of glasses.

My mother said, "I will identify the body."

My father turned and put his hand over hers.

"I'll do it," she said, quietly.

"I don't think that will be necessary, Mrs. Buchanan," said the coroner.

And then he left us alone, my mother beside me, trembling, but not crying, burying her face in a Kleenex like someone seeing how long she could hold her breath.

"There's some water," said the woman behind glass.

It was an Arrowhead Springs bottle and a dispenser, with a metal cylinder and paper cups. I tugged the bottom cup, and another cup fell immediately into place, ready for the next thirsty person. I tried to think like this, step by step.

I plunged the handle and the paper cup filled with cold water. It was more than cold—it was very nearly ice. A bubble burned up from within the glass urn of water. I gave the cup to my mother, who did not see it until some of it pattered onto the floor, and then she drank.

32

● ● ● ● ● ●

They were turned toward each other, what they weren't saying between them like a package they were protecting, invisible but easy to break. I put my foot out idly, as though I found the floor fascinating, into a faded place in the tile where they must have had a potted plant, but an artificial one. There were no windows.

Fear turns into a numb fever after a while. But that makes it more bearable. Just as the wait was beginning to paralyze us so we couldn't feel anything, the door to the inside opened.

Detective Waterman looked like her own sister, someone less sure of herself, a wrinkle down either side of her mouth. "They are going to take just a few minutes," she said.

"A few minutes," said my mother in a quiet, determined voice.

Detective Waterman buttoned her sweater, her

blouse hanging out under the fisherman's knit. So it wasn't just me, I thought. It *was* cold in here.

"They don't do anything quickly in this place," said Detective Waterman, making a polite expression of pain to show that she cared. I wondered if that was how the English teacher Detective Waterman would have acted if she had to tell Senior English their term papers fell into the swimming pool.

Her hand searched for the doorknob. The blouse hanging down beneath the sweater was pink, a smock bunched against her body by the sweater. I wondered if Detective Waterman might be pregnant. "But I'll go see if I can't speed them up a little." She didn't move, maybe waiting for us to excuse her.

"What kind of clothes was the body wearing?" said my mother, keeping her voice strong. You could hardly guess her feelings.

"There were no clothes." The detective paused for a split second, a little wrinkle of pain. "Sometimes when they search downhill later on, they find clothes."

"Earrings," said my mother. Anita had gotten her ears pierced when she was thirteen. My father hated the idea of pierced ears; my mother thought it was inevitable. A shop on Union Square in San Francisco did the hole-punching while I looked on, women with long sparkling fingernails saying what a wide range of choices Anita would have.

"There's no apparent jewelry," said the detective.

My mother and I could take a sifter and a tub and go up to Skyline. If there was a turquoise stud up there, we would find it.

I thought my mother was going to ask whether the lobes were pierced, but I thought: skunks, rats. Maybe coyotes. I knew why they couldn't simply take fingerprints. Mentally I begged my mother to stop asking.

We were alone.

My father was out of his chair, touching the doorknob, listening against the interior door.

The woman behind the chicken-wire glass leaned way over, trying to see him, but he was out of her range of vision. My father's voice sounded detached from what he was doing, pacing crazily, lunging to test the door again. "We'll start a new chapter of Find the Children," he said. "Focus on kids from the Bay Area. We'll have the faces of these kids on billboards, BART, everywhere. People won't be able to go out for a dozen eggs without seeing them."

This was typical of my dad. He never ate eggs, hated them. But he thought of other people, normal people, as being unlike him in subtle ways, not caring about cholesterol. I had always thought my father assumed he was more competent than most people, but was nice about it, feeling it made him all the more responsible for what happened.

Gradually the woman behind the glass got used to him and didn't bother watching him as he paced.

"We'll make it impossible for people to forget. Physically impossible."

Detective Waterman had trouble getting into the room, and my father helped her, holding the door. She was carrying Anita's X rays, black comic strips.

"It's not Anita," said the detective.

But her statement was canceled by the sound of the door gasping as it swung back, the entire building full of heavy doors that wouldn't open and wouldn't shut.

"There is no question," said Detective Waterman, her voice rising a little. "It's someone else."

I waited, not wanting to be relieved too soon.

"I personally," said my mother, "want to verify that whoever you have in that room is not my daughter."

That froze everyone. "I'm sorry I brought you all the way down here," said the detective.

My grandmother makes the same bitter smile, wise to everything. "I want to see the body," said my mother.

Dad put his hand out, to her shoulder. He gave his head a small shake, left, right, looking hard into her eyes.

Detective Waterman had trouble yanking a paper cup from the dispenser. "Anita had very good teeth," she said.

"Fluoride," said my dad. "It's putting dentists out of business." That's what he was saying. But I knew what he felt.

Detective Waterman did not drink, just watched it sloshing around the small paper cup. "The body we recovered has extensive dental work."

"So," my mother said.

We all waited.

"She can't be Anita," said my mother at last.

I put my arm around her. Her feelings were inside, a hive.

"It was a good idea for you to have them on file," said the detective, her voice husky. "It saved some time."

"It's because I know how hard it is," said my mother softly after a long silence. She spent a lot of time being patient with people. "If you find something. Sometimes you don't know what it is."

It was almost dark outside, the neon coroner's light stuttering on, all the neon tubing bright except for the *r* at the end. The air was warm, and sounds were too loud, car doors slamming, a motorcycle puttering by in the street.

"When did you get her dental records?" said my father.

"A few days after it happened," she said. She didn't get into the Jeep, just leaned against it as another coroner's van squeezed past, its yellow light flashing

"I wish you'd told me," he said, on his side of the Jeep, toying with the keys as though he found them intriguing. "It's like—"

"What's it like, Derrick?" she asked. "You mean it was like I was losing hope?"

My dad didn't say anything.

We all got into the Jeep, and Dad backed it all the way out into the street and up to the intersection before he remembered to turn on the headlights. And then he had to pull over to the side of the street and wait for his composure to come back.

It was full darkness, stoplights and car lights bright, but far off, nothing real. We were all the way up Lincoln Avenue when I saw them, the red police flashers. I said, "Dad, how fast are we going?" as a hint.

He said, "Oh, Christ," and pulled over to the curb.

The police car parked right where I could get an eyeful of flashing red.

Dad got his driver's license out and the cop took it, shining his light on it, the size of a pen with a bright ray illuminating the cop's wedding ring, my dad's profile. "When were you thinking of taking care of that muffler?" the cop asked.

"I got used to that racket," said my dad, sounding tired but perky. "Didn't even hear it after a while."

The cop looked at the license, a brilliant white slip in his pink fingers, the flashlight so bright.

"I could hear you four blocks away," said the cop.

"This is undeniably possible," said my dad.

The cop was thinking, heavy, cube-shaped cop thoughts. He pointed the light in at my mother, back at me. "You haven't by any chance been drinking, Mr. Buchanan?"

I should have waited. Because then he straightened a little, maybe recalling the name, making sense of who we were, but it was too late.

I was out of the back of the Jeep, around the cab, face-to-face with the cop, and telling him he should know who these people were.

The cop putting his fingers on my chest, all ten of them, trying to push me away without putting any strength into it, my dad saying, "Cray, get back in the car."

That night I could hear my mother, locked in the bathroom next to my parent's bedroom. She was talking to Anita, as though Anita were there in the house, asking Anita where she was.

33

● ● ● ● ● ●

We drove up to Lake Tahoe to shut up our cabin for the winter.

That wasn't the only reason. There was something we had to check again for ourselves.

We had an easy ride, new muffler and new seat cushions, and Dad had them put an all-weather shell over the vehicle, enclosing it so I didn't feel like a prisoner of war sitting in the back watching the traffic on Interstate 80. I told myself I had liked it better before, strapped in and hanging on.

But I liked it better this way, the Jeep almost like a family car now. It was early October, and my parents sat in the front seat listening to Stanford get slaughtered by the University of Arizona while I stared down the receding lanes of traffic, the floodplain of the Yolo Causeway, empty and stripped of crops this time of year, Sacramento, off-ramps and motels, and then the foothills, oak trees twisting out of the rocky slopes. All the way looking backward, not getting drowsy for even a moment, until by near sunset we were whipping along the Sierra two-lane, a margin of a little snow on either side of the road, patches under the pines.

We had not visited all summer. We had paid only one visit that year, during Easter week for one night, shaking out the hammock, sweeping the spiders out of the kitchen, Anita telling us that an exoskeleton wouldn't mend like human bones.

The doctor had said my dad was about to have a blooming ulcer again. That's the way Dr. Pollock expressed himself, according to my father. "Blooming ulcer," like a British cop in a black-and-white movie, an old codger sipping tea, the blooming rainy weather, the blooming Jerries, dropping bombs all over London. But we knew what the doctor meant, how the secret sore might open up, like a flower. Ever since the evening at the coroner's bureau, and the eventual news that the body was a young woman from Portland, Oregon, we had been needing to go somewhere far from home.

When Dad found first gear, the new clutch like a miracle, we jackrabbited up the drive, over the boulders barely submerged under the pine needles, and I was the first one out of the car, into air that was still warm, a little summer returning before winter came for good.

———

We had hoped, only half aware of it.

We needed to be sure. The sheriff's department had checked the cabin right after we reported Anita gone, and periodically over the last three months they had continued to drop by the place.

Once we had come up to find signs of a break-in, the bottle of Wild Turkey Dad had kept under the sink empty and abandoned on the back porch, the denim shirts, hiking boots, and lumberjack shirts rifled, but nothing missing.

I unlocked the cabin door with a key of my own, and let the door swing inward.

The cabin was exactly as all four of us had left it, the cans of mushroom soup unopened, the extra long wooden fireplace matches, the yellowing want ads under a splintery chunk of wood, the amber red sap that had leaked out of the firewood last March grown white and stiff.

My dad marched across the room and grabbed the phone there by the breakfast bar, taking a seat on the stool and calling up the answering machine. He didn't bother telling us what the messages were, just listened, licking his lips, all of us breathing a little hard.

"I can see why mountain climbers carry oxygen," puffed my mother, the seven thousand feet of altitude hitting her especially. "I see spots," she said. "In front of my eyes." She waved her hand, parting gnats, except that there was nothing there.

She fell onto the sofa with an apologetic laugh. Dad gave us his no-news expression, lips together, eyes focused on nothing. He hung up the phone. He said he would try to get the heater going, but I could tell that he needed to do something, anything, all of us struck by the hope we had never expressed, crazy, stupid, completely illogical. A hope that was suddenly gone.

There was no sign of a visit from Anita anywhere, not even in the bathroom with the glass shelves of the medicine cabinet that were always cold, even in the middle of summer, retaining a trace of the winter freeze. Things were like that in the mountains. Opening a closet, rummaging for slippers, when I found one it was like iron, cold footwear that had not been warm for months, another one of her shoes.

Anita's old traces were everywhere, including books she had long since outgrown, biographies of great female athletes, women of science. There was an empty forty-five pistol shell beside the blue scrub jay feather. I remembered when Anita found the copper shell, picking it up, carrying it back to the cabin, a thing that did not belong.

"I didn't realize she had so many clothes here," said my father, the heater huffing on at last. "That's why I had to turn right around and come out here. I look and see a line of hiking boots and running shoes, all of them hers." Shoes she had outgrown, I nearly said.

The counselor we had been seeing had encouraged us to share our feelings.

Dad turned a knob on the heater and shut the door. He locked it, to keep the raccoons out. He found his way out over the roots of a sugar pine, taking deep breaths. He put his hand out to steady himself against a tree. "You told me it was a bad idea to come up here, that I ought to have the management company take care of the mouse holes and nail the shutters."

"I didn't say it was a bad idea." I had asked, "Are you sure?"

"We'll tool on up there and winterize the cabin," was the way he had put it. If he didn't get rest soon, he would need blood, type A, bleeding inside the way he had when he was younger and the market for wicker chairs collapsed. I couldn't help reminding myself that the nearest hospital was in Tahoe City.

When he stood silent for too long, I could sense the emptiness grow in him. He put his hand out to a sprig of pine, needing to touch something.

"Did you think she might have come here?" my dad asked.

"Maybe I did. In the back of my mind," I said.

"Maybe she did show up," he said. He never used to sound like this. "And she was very careful not to disturb anything."

"Dad, I think I'm going to go for a swim." Just to distract him, give him something to think about.

"It's almost dark," he said.

"It'll be invigorating."

A swim in that water could kill a person, too far from shore. The water in Lake Tahoe was always just a few degrees above turning into ice, year-round. The lake never actually froze. It stayed just the way it was. But it was a tradition in our family, a quick dive in the water, an hour by the fire. It was late in the year for it, snow like dirty napkins out by the gravel drive, but the air was still warm, scented with sugar pine.

My mother was still breathing hard, leaning back on the sofa. She saw me whisk my bathing trunks out of the duffel bag and she said, "Cray, you're a maniac." But it was after a moment's hesitation, after she was going to say something else. This happened a lot, these days. Even when the fax came, saying that she could name her new species of bay tree, she didn't tell us. I had to find out about it going through her papers, throwing away the mail she said God had not given her the strength to read.

My bare feet felt their way, down along the pine twigs and the ant holes I could still see in the near dark, as though the sun had begun to set and then rebounded, bouncing gently back for an extra few minutes of dusk.

"It's almost freezing," my dad said, teasingly, like a little kid, someone who wanted to be liked. Sometimes I felt this about my father—what a nervous, eager little kid he must have been, dancing around when he got all his spelling words right.

He probably couldn't see me against the dark water, shuddering not so much with cold but because the sand down near the lake was granite meal, coarse, and pinecones skittered underfoot. I half stepped on one, getting a pine tooth stuck under the ball of my foot, stuck on with pine sap.

The lake crept up to my ankles, and I stood still. The mountains rose up, all the way around the lake, like outlines that had not existed one minute before. Little prickles of light distracted my eye, the casinos on the Nevada side.

My leg bones ached. I told myself I would get used to it, taking another step, up to my knees, shivering. "It's not too bad," I called out, wondering if my dad was still watching, wanting him to be, hoping he would come down to the edge of the lake.

I shook my foot to get the pine tooth off my sole, but I could not feel it. I couldn't feel anything.

"So what do you think?" said my dad from somewhere behind me, close. "Do you think I ought to go in and get my suit on, and come down for a swim?"

I thought he might be joking, but then he said, "I have those old bathing trunks with the starfish printed on them, remember?" I could tell he was not joking, and yet he wasn't serious either. He was just talking, needing to hear whatever I would say.

"No, I don't think you better," I said.

I could hear him thinking about my words, taking another step, looking out at me, or past me, at the water. I could feel him wanting to dive in, and swim as far and as hard as he could. I could feel him needing to hear my voice.

"I think you're right," I said. "It's too cold."

I knew he was looking at me, trying to see me in the dark.